THE FATAL FURY

"Can't go back the way you came, Adams," a voice shouted . . .

"Who are you?" Clint called out.

"Me? I'm the man who's gonna kill the famous Gunsmith."

"You got a name?"

There was a moment of silence, then the man answered, "It's Duncan."

"Never heard of you," Clint called out.

"That's okay," Duncan said. "I'm gonna kill you, anyway."

"Well, come ahead, then," Clint told him. "Let's get it over with . . ."

DON'T MISS THESE
ALL-ACTION WESTERN SERIES
FROM THE BERKLEY PUBLISHING GROUP

THE GUNSMITH by J. R. Roberts
 Clint Adams was a legend among lawmen, outlaws, and ladies. They called him . . . the Gunsmith.

LONGARM by Tabor Evans
 The popular long-running series about U.S. Deputy Marshal Long—his life, his loves, his fight for justice.

LONE STAR by Wesley Ellis
 The blazing adventures of Jessica Starbuck and the martial arts master, Ki. Over eight million copies in print.

SLOCUM by Jake Logan
 Today's longest-running action Western. John Slocum rides a deadly trail of hot blood and cold steel.

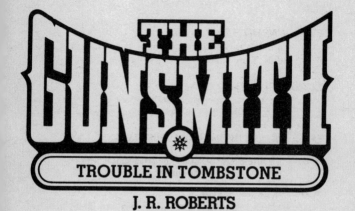

THE GUNSMITH

TROUBLE IN TOMBSTONE

J. R. ROBERTS

JOVE BOOKS, NEW YORK

TROUBLE IN TOMBSTONE

A Jove Book / published by arrangement with
the author

PRINTING HISTORY
Jove edition / October 1993

ISBN: 0-515-11212-7

A JOVE BOOK®
Jove Books are published by The Berkley Publishing Group,
200 Madison Avenue, New York, New York 10016.
JOVE and the "J" design are trademarks
belonging to Jove Publications, Inc.

PRINTED IN THE UNITED STATES OF AMERICA

10 9 8 7 6 5 4 3 2 1

PROLOGUE

EL PASO, TEXAS

Texas, New Mexico and Old Mexico all came together in one small little section of land called El Paso. Because this created a cross section of cultures and politics, El Paso presented problems like no other town in Texas. For one thing, outlaws who were wanted on one side or the other of the border had only to cross it to escape capture. For another thing, El Paso was an isolated section of Texas, and that isolation attracted lawbreakers.

For this reason El Paso was largely lawless, and while the town fathers could count on the Texas Rangers for *some* help, this did not solve the problem entirely.

The town fathers, in their search for a town tamer, advertised that they wanted a man who was sober, discreet and fearless. In early 1881 such a man was hired at the salary of one hundred dollars a month.

His name was Dallas Stoudenmire.

Stoudenmire was a gunfighter. He was six-foot-two, long legged and auburn haired, with a love of living that sometimes got the better of him. He liked liquor, and women, but he was serious about his job as marshal. He was also extremely proud. And when it came to keeping the peace, Stoudenmire depended on his ability with a gun more often than not.

In an El Paso full of gamblers, prostitutes, cattlemen, soldiers and miners, Stoudenmire went about his job with such verve that he made many enemies. The Texas Rangers did not like him. The Manning brothers, who controlled all gambling and prostitution in El Paso, feuded with him from almost the very beginning. Politicians feared him. More than one assassination attempt was made on Stoudenmire, and there were any number of suspects who might have initiated them.

It was into this El Paso that Clint Adams rode, and he had no idea how much violence and death lay ahead of him.

PART
ONE

~

EL PASO, TEXAS
APRIL 14, 1881

ONE

When Clint Adams rode into El Paso, Texas, it was for a very simple reason—he had never been there before.

He'd been sitting in his friend Rick Hartman's saloon, Rick's Place, in Labyrinth, Texas, listening to some cowboys at the bar talk about El Paso. They had alternately called it "wide open," "fun," and a "hellhole." They'd also said something, though, about a new lawman who was already making people nervous.

When Clint had told Hartman he was going to take a ride over to El Paso, his friend had frowned at him and asked, "For Godsake, why?"

And Clint had told him.

"Well, I never been to Hell either," Hartman had said, in reply, "but I'm sure not looking forward to it."

"El Paso is not quite Hell," Clint had answered.

"You run along, then," Hartman had said. "I'll

5

stay right here where I know it's safe ... and
profitable. You can tell me all about it when you
get back ... *if* you get back."

The next morning, Clint had left for El Paso.

He'd had some idea of where El Paso was,
but hadn't realized it was virtually on the border between Texas, New Mexico and Mexico.

As he rode into town Clint could immediately
see what the cowboys in Rick's Place had meant.
El Paso had the look of a wide open town.
Many of the buildings were adobe, and many of
them seemed to be saloons or gambling establish-
ments. Where there were no buildings—adobe or
otherwise—there were haphazardly erected prostitutes' cribs.

The streets were wet from a recent downpour.
When Clint reached the intersection of El Paso
and San Antonio streets the mire was so deep
that his big black gelding, Duke, had to pull his
large hooves free with wet, sucking sounds.

Here and there he spotted men leaning against
a wall or a post, most of them wearing low-slung
gunbelts and watching him from heavy-lidded
eyes. El Paso had the definite feel of a town
where everyone was out for what he could get.

Riding into town from the north, Clint had
passed an area posted as the future site of tracks
for the Southern Pacific Railroad. If the denizens
of El Paso thought the town was wild and wide
open now, wait until they saw what the presence
of the railroad would do to it. In Clint's experience,

the railroad had made some towns, and been the ruination of others.

He found the livery stable and gave over Duke into the hands of the liveryman, who gave him directions to a hotel. "You'll get honest rates there," the man said, "and clean sheets."

"Clean?" Clint asked.

The man grinned a gap-toothed grin—and he was young, still in his twenties—and said, "Well, cleaner than most places."

Clint took his saddlebags and rifle and headed for the hotel. He was almost out the door when he turned and called out, "Hey, who's the law around here?"

"Stoudenmire," the man answered, "Marshal Dallas Stoudenmire."

"Stoudenmire," Clint repeated to himself, shaking his head. "Don't know him."

"We didn't, either," the man said. "He's been marshal here a few months, though, and we all knows him now. Do we ever!"

Clint thought that Marshal Dallas Stoudenmire must have made an impact on El Paso. He thought he might like to meet the man who could do that in this town.

Clint checked into the hotel the liveryman had directed him to. It was a small adobe building with all the rooms on one floor. He walked to the end of a corridor behind the desk and opened the door to his room. Looking at the bed, he thought, if the sheets were *supposed* to be gray, they were probably clean.

The furnishings in the room were simple. A
bed, a small table with a pitcher and basin on
it, and that was it. He was willing to bet that
some of the whores' stalls were more comfortable
than this.

He dropped his saddlebags on the bed, leaned
his rifle against the wall, then turned and left the
room. At the desk Clint asked directions to the
Marshal's office. It usually worked in his favor to
let the law know he was in town, rather than letting them discover it for themselves. He walked
over there to introduce himself and announce his
arrival.

The marshal's office was another small adobe
building, this one with a heavy wooden door.
Clint knocked and entered. Behind the desk sat
a stern-jawed man in his late thirties, looking at
him curiously as he entered and closed the door
behind him.

"Marshal Stoudenmire?" Clint asked.

"That's me," Stoudenmire answered. "Who're
you?"

"My name's Clint Adams, Marshal."

"Adams," Stoudenmire said, raising his eye-
brows now. "The Gunsmith."

"That's right."

"What brings you to El Paso, Mr. Adams?"

Clint gave Stoudenmire the same answer he
had given Rick Hartman. "I've never been here,"
Clint said. "Heard a lot about it, though."

"No doubt," Stoudenmire said, "you've heard
what a wide open town this is."

"That, and more," Clint responded. "I heard they had a tough lawman here."

"Well . . . that remains to be seen, I guess," Stoudenmire said. "I'm doin' my best here, is all I know."

"That's all you can do, isn't it?"

The marshal nodded. "Seems to me I heard you were a lawman some years back," he said.

Clint smiled. "A lot of years ago, is more like it."

"Well, you know what it's like, then," Stoudenmire said. "I'd appreciate it if you weren't intent on making it worse on me while you're here."

"Not me, Marshal," Clint replied. "That's why I wanted to come over and announce myself. I want to make sure you know I'm not here to cause trouble."

"I appreciate the visit, then, Mr. Adams," Stoudenmire said. "Fact is, maybe later tonight I can buy you a drink at the Top Dollar Saloon."

"Top Dollar?"

Stoudenmire nodded. "Decent place," he said. "Only one in town not owned or run by the Mannings."

"The Mannings," Clint mused. "Don't think I know them. More than one, are there?"

Stoudenmire grinned now. "Frank, James, John, William and Doc Manning."

"Doc?"

"That's Felix," Stoudenmire said. "He's a doctor. The other four, they run everything around here.

The saloons, the whorehouses, the gambling, even some rustling, though I can't prove that."

"Sound like a bad lot."

Stoudenmire frowned.

"Some of them are all right, really; it's just that they and I . . . well, some folks hereabouts call it a feud. Me, I don't look at it that way."

"Well, El Paso sure doesn't sound like a boring place," Clint said.

"No, that's for sure," Stoudenmire agreed. "It's never boring around here. We got all kinds here, and we got everything a man could want—everything that ain't good for 'im, you know?"

"I know," Clint said.

"Well," said Stoudenmire. "Thanks for comin' over. I'll be over to the Top Dollar in a few hours."

"I'll look for you there," Clint replied.

As Clint headed for the door Stoudenmire asked, "How long you plannin' on stayin' in town, Mr. Adams?"

Clint opened the door and stopped. "I hadn't planned, actually," he said. "I guess I'll just see what happens."

Stoudenmire nodded and then looked down at the top of his desk.

Clint took that as a dismissal and left.

After Clint Adams left, Stoudenmire stood up and walked over to the one window his office had. He looked outside and watched Clint crossing the street.

He knew Adams' reputation, but he also knew

that the further they spread, the more reputations were blown out of proportion. All he knew for sure was that Adams was good with a gun. He wondered idly if the man was just taking a look at El Paso, as he had said, or if he was here because he'd been hired by the Mannings.

Like a lot of things, he supposed that remained to be seen.

TWO

Because Stoudenmire had mentioned the place, Clint Adams went to the Top Dollar Saloon first. It wasn't much of a place, small and cramped, the bar fashioned from wooden planks on top of some barrels. The bartender looked bored, leaning on the planks and staring off into space. There were five or six tables in the place, and there was a lone man seated at one.

Maybe, Clint thought, this is what places *not* run by the Mannings look like.

He walked over to the bar. The bartender seemed sort of startled as he straightened up.

"How about a beer?" Clint asked.

"Comin' up," the barkeep said.

When it came the beer was good and cold.

"Place isn't too busy, is it?" Clint asked.

"Never is," replied the bartender.

"Why's that?"

"Plenty of other places in town that offer more

12

than just good beer," the man said.

"Like what?"

"Gamblin', and girls."

"Looks like I could go anywhere on the street and get a girl," Clint said.

"Sure," the man answered, "and a disease. You want a girl who won't make your dick fall off, in this town you go to the Mannings."

"The Mannings?"

"Yeah," the bartender said, "they own almost everything else in town except for this place."

"Who owns this place?"

The man made a pained face. "I do."

"Why don't you sell out?"

"Who'd buy?"

"I hear the marshal drinks here."

The man looked pained again. "That's another reason we're never busy," he said. "If he'd drink someplace else, I might have more customers. Nobody wants to get between him and a bullet, you know what I mean?"

"I think so."

The man leaned his elbows on the makeshift bar and stared off into space again. Clint finished his beer and left. Now he wanted to see what a Manning-owned saloon looked like.

The most conspicuous place on the street was called the Coliseum Saloon and Variety Theatre, but it looked more like a barn than a saloon or a theater. The establishment had nine rooms and offered all forms of entertainment, from the the-

atrical to what might be called the more personal.
Gambling, whores, drinking, it was all available
at the Coliseum.

When Clint entered, a well-dressed man in his
twenties asked him what his pleasure was.

"Right now," Clint said, "all I would like is a
drink and an opportunity to look around—if that's
all right?"

"Sir," the young man replied, "at the Coliseum
anything you want to do is all right with us."

"As long as I pay for it, naturally," Clint said.

"Well . . . ," the man looked flustered, "of
course."

"Of course," Clint repeated. "Which way do I
go?"

"Uh, straight ahead, sir," the man said, still
frowning. "Right into the main saloon."

"Thanks."

Clint went through the doorway indicated and
found himself in a huge room with a high ceiling,
crystal chandeliers, gaming tables and the longest
bar he had ever seen, upholstered in red leather
with metal studs. It was before suppertime, and
the place was about three quarters full already.
What it would look like after dinner, and after
dark, was anybody's guess. Clint doubted that
anyone coming in late would be able to find an
empty table to sit at, or a space at a gaming table
or the bar.

Impressed, Clint descended three steps into the
main saloon and walked up to the bar. He leaned
an elbow on the bartop and watched as one of the

two red-vested bartenders approached to take his order.

"Beer," he said, and then added, "Please."

"Comin' up, sir," the bartender said.

Both bartenders were young, dark haired, slender, probably hired for their looks more than anything else. They went well with the rest of the place.

The bartender served him his beer and he took a sip. It was ice cold, as had been the one he'd had at the Top Dollar. The beer was the same, but the ambience was certainly different.

Clint turned, beer mug in hand, and took a closer look at the place.

It was filled with beautiful women, and they all worked there. Some of them were dressed in gaily colored gowns, cut low to show generous cleavage and smooth, sometimes creamy skin. These were the gals who were working the floor, serving drinks and flirting with the customers.

About half of the dealers at the gaming tables were also women. Not dressed as provocatively as the saloon girls, they were nevertheless attractive and would be an obvious distraction to all but the most serious of gamblers.

He turned and beckoned to the bartender.

"Yes, sir?"

"Who owns this place?"

"Why . . . the Mannings, sir. That is, Mr. Jim and Mr. John Manning."

"Aren't there more than two Mannings?"

"Yes, sir," the man said. "Frank, he owns his own saloon."

"I see."

"Can I get you another beer, sir?"

"No," Clint said, "thanks. I'll keep working on this one."

"You're a stranger in town, aren't you?" the bartender asked.

"Yes." Probably anyone who didn't know that the Mannings owned the Coliseum had to be a stranger, Clint figured. "Arrived today," he added.

"I thought so," the man said. "Gonna stay long?"

"I don't know," Clint answered. "I guess that depends on how I like the town, doesn't it?"

"I suppose so, sir," replied the bartender. "Excuse me." He went off to serve another new arrival.

Clint finished his beer and decided that he was hungry. The little hotel he was staying in certainly had no dining room. *This* place, he thought, would definitely have a restaurant, but he wasn't sure yet that he wanted to eat in a Manning-owned place. He wondered idly if he'd be able to find a place to eat that the Mannings didn't own.

Clint put his empty mug down on the bar and left the Coliseum, feeling that he had not done enough—or dressed well enough—to do the place justice.

As Clint Adams left the Coliseum the bartender he had been talking to, Sam Jones, waved over one of the saloon girls.

"Who was the good-looking guy you were talkin' to, Sam?" Elaine Mills asked.

"Never mind, Elaine," Sam said to the pert blonde. "Find me Mr. Manning."

"Which one?" She leaned on the bar lazily. Normally he would have taken the time to look down her dress. This time, however, he barely noticed.

"It don't matter," Sam said. "I got to talk to one of them, is all."

"Whataya want me to tell 'im?"

Sam gave her a look. "Tell one of them I got to talk to him!"

"All right, all right," she said, "you don't have to get so testy. I'll do it."

"Do it fast, then," Sam retorted. "I got some news, and they're gonna want to know about it."

"What news?"

Sam closed his eyes for a moment, then opened them and glared at her. "Just do it, Elaine!"

She gave him a mock look of horror. "I'm goin', I'm goin'. You know, you ain't so damn scary, Sam Jones."

Maybe *he* wasn't scary, Sam thought as she hurried off, but the man who had just left the Coliseum sure was. Sam hadn't recognized him first off, but the second time, when the man had asked the questions about who owned the place, that was when he recognized him.

Clint Adams, the Gunsmith.

The Mannings were gonna be real interested to hear that he was in town.

THREE

Clint had been going to a little cafe on San Antonio Street. It wasn't busy, but he'd learned that it was never really bust, either. The food wasn't that good, but it was run by a husband and wife, and the coffee was good and strong. That he had found out immediately, because the first thing he'd ordered was a pot of coffee.

When the woman first started waiting on him, he hadn't known that she and her husband ran the place. All he knew was that she was attractive. She had long, dark hair and pale skin that showed she spent very little time outdoors. Her hands betrayed the fact that she worked hard, but that was the last thing he would ever hold against a woman.

She wasn't young—probably in her mid-thirties—but the age of a woman never bothered him. He'd made love to women of all ages, and found that how old they were had very little to do with

how much he enjoyed them. What years did add
to a woman was experience, and that he was usually grateful for. There were times when he didn't
want to instruct, and times when he didn't mind
guiding a girl who wasn't so experienced.

"My name's Wynona," the woman said when he
entered. "What can I get you?"

"Coffee," Clint answered.

"How do you like it?"

"Black and strong."

"Comin' up."

He watched her walk to the kitchen, enjoying
the way she moved. No nonsense about her walk,
and yet her full hips and well padded butt moved
enticingly.

The older Clint got, the more he enjoyed the
company of women. It didn't even matter if he
went to bed with them or not. He just liked
watching them, talking to them, being near them,
smelling them—and then if they went to bed, well,
that was a bonus.

He enjoyed watching this Wynona walk back
and forth from the kitchen with his coffee, and
his biscuits, and finally with his steak platter.

She came by as he was sawing through his
meat and smiled at him.

"A little tough for you?"

"Some," he admitted.

"But the coffee's good, huh?"

"The coffee's very good," he agreed, taking up
his cup. "Good coffee makes up for a lot."

"My Jake, he ain't much for cookin'," she said,

"but I'm even worse. We both make good coffee, though."

"Your Jake?"

"Yeah." She made a rueful face. "We're married . . . sorta."

"What does sorta mean?"

"Well," the woman said, "basically it means I'm married when it suits me."

"And when does it not suit you?"

"Well," she said again, laying a hand on his arm, "usually when some good-lookin' stranger comes to town and watches me real close when I walk back and forth."

Clint colored slightly, something he rarely did. "You noticed," he said. "I'm sorry."

"Don't be," she responded. Her hand on his arm seemed to grow warmer. "A woman likes when a man admires her, and watches her."

"I like to watch women," Clint admitted.

"Do you like to do *more* than watch?" she asked, eyeing him in a way that was not just playful. Her question was dead serious.

"I do," he answered, "but usually when they're *not* married."

"Oh," she said, "you let somethin' like that stop you, do you?"

"I do," Clint replied, then surprised himself by adding, "sometimes."

"Oh," the woman said, finally removing her hand, "that's good to know. What's your name?"

"Clint," he answered. "Clint Adams."

"Well, Clint Adams," she continued, "my full

name's Wynona Jamison. Um, how long you plannin' on bein' in town, exactly?"

"Long enough, I reckon," Clint said, surprising himself further. Well, what of it? She *said* she was only sort of married, didn't she? And he *had* been riding a horse for a long time. As much as he enjoyed the company of his big gelding, Duke, there came a time in a man's life when he needed some female company.

"Stayin' at the hotel?" Wynona asked.

"Yes."

"Well," she said, "enjoy your meal, and I hope you enjoy the rest of your stay."

"I plan to."

"Good." She smiled at him. "I like a man with a plan."

She walked away, not looking to see if he was watching her. She *knew* he was, of course, and what he liked was that she still did not alter her walk. No showy hip twitching for Wynona Jamison.

He thought that they probably understood each other.

Clint ate the rest of his meal slowly, had a second pot of coffee, then paid his bill and walked over to the Top Dollar. When he passed her his money, their hands met, and lingered.

They understood each other very well.

FOUR

Jim Manning sat behind his desk, while his brother John stood next to it. The desk was Jim's because getting into the saloon business had been his idea. He had done it first—before John, that is. It was Frank, with his Frank's Saloon, who had actually gotten into the business first. Jim had opened his first saloon without John, though, and then they had opened the Coliseum together. They shared the office and the desk, but when they were both in the room at the same time it was Jim who sat at the desk.

There was a knock on the door. John called out, "Come in."

The door opened and the bartender, Sam Jones, stepped in.

"Mr. Manning," he said, bobbing his head at Jim. Then he looked at John and added awkwardly, "Uh . . . Mr. Manning."

"What's on your mind, Sam?" Jim asked. "You sent one of the girls to find us, but you didn't tell her what it was about."

"No, sir," Sam said. "I didn't think she had to know the, uh, whole story."

"And just what is the whole story, Sam?" John Manning asked.

"Well, sir, a man came into the place today," the bartender answered. "He had a beer, asked some questions about you, and then left."

"About me specifically?" Jim asked, jerking his thumb at his chest.

"Uh, about the Mannings . . . sir."

"Who was the man, Sam?" John asked. "Did you know him?"

"Well, not right off," Sam said, "not at first. But then when he was talkin', I realized who he was. See, I was real small when I seen him the first time, but I remember him."

The Manning brothers exchanged a glance. Jim asked, "Why is that, Sam? Why do you remember him so well after all that time?"

"I ain't never seen one man kill four before, Mr. Manning," Sam said to Jim Manning. "Not in a fair fight, anyway."

The Mannings exchanged another glance, and Jim leaned forward in his chair. "You saw one man kill four men . . . in a fair gunfight?" he asked.

"Yes, sir."

"Who was the man, Sam?"

Sam looked at both brothers in turn, then stared at Jim Manning as he answered. "Clint Adams, sir. They call him the Gunsmith."

• • •

When Clint entered the Top Dollar Saloon he saw the same man who had been there before, still sitting at the same table. In fact, it even seemed that he had the same drink in front of him.

"Doesn't he ever move?" he asked the bartender, jerking a thumb at the man.

"Only when he farts," the bartender said, wiping the dirty bartop with an even dirtier rag. "Makes him rise up some, is all. What'll it be for ya?"

"Beer."

The man nodded, drew a beer and placed it in front of Clint with a bored look on his face. With nothing to do, he leaned his elbows on the bar and made conversation.

"Did you get to see any of the other places in town?" he asked.

"Just the Coliseum."

"Jeez, that's enough," the bartender said, rolling his eyes. "And you came back here?"

Clint grinned at the man. "There's something more honest, more . . . oh, down to earth, about this place."

"You kiddin' me?" the man asked. He squinted, peering closely at Clint to see if he was pulling his leg.

"Nope."

"You ain't gettin' a beer on the house, ya know," the man said. "I can't afford it."

"I'll pay."

The man stared at Clint for a moment, then

nodded, though he still looked suspicious.

"The marshal been in yet?" Clint asked.

"No," the bartender said. "Why?"

"Oh, he said something about meeting me here."

"Can I ask you . . . are you, uh, friends with the marshal?"

Clint shook his head. "Just met him today."

"And he wants to buy you a drink already?"

"I guess that's true, yeah."

The bartender leaned his elbows on the bar, stroked his chin thoughtfully and said, "That makes you the closest thing to a friend he's got in this town since Doc Cummings got killed."

"Doc Cummings?" Clint queried.

"You think you could, uh, get him to drink somewheres else?" the bartender asked hopefully, ignoring his question.

"Why?"

"I get sort of nervous, havin' a man with a bullseye on his back drinkin' in my place."

"All lawmen walk around with a bullseye on their backs," Clint said.

"Not like this one," the bartender said. "I really wish you could convince him. Think you can?"

"I might."

"Really?"

"Tell me about Doc Cummings," Clint said, "and I'll see what I can do."

The man stroked his jaw for a few moments, thinking that over.

"What's wrong?" asked Clint.

"Well, if the marshal was to find out that I was talking about Doc Cummings, I don't think he'd take it very kindly."

"Well," replied Clint, "I'm not going to tell him if you don't."

"Well—"

"I'll even buy another beer," Clint offered, and then added, "or three."

The man's face brightened. "You got a deal, friend."

FIVE

Some said, the bartender began, that Dallas Stoudenmire and Doc Cummings were related, maybe by marriage. Nobody knew for sure. All that was known was that they were close friends and that both were dangerous men. In fact, they were both ex–Texas Rangers.

Years later they came together in El Paso, Stoudenmire as the marshal, Cummings as a successful restauranteur. In fact, Cummings had opened several restaurants in El Paso, and they had all been successful. The most famous one was called The Globe, located on El Paso Street.

The two men were enough alike to be brothers. They were hard drinkers, with a strong belief in right and wrong—and an even stronger belief that *they* were never wrong. They were not above killing to make a point, they were hard pressed to ever forgive a wrong done them, and they were extremely loyal—especially to each other.

So it was no surprise that Doc Cummings

backed Dallas Stoudenmire every step of the way in his feud with the Manning brothers. He had become especially incensed when there was an attempt to assassinate Dallas Stoudenmire. Although the marshal survived, he was laid up for a while, and it was then that Cummings decided that the Mannings—specifically Jim—had been behind the attempt. During an earlier shootout Stoudenmire had killed two men who were friends of the Mannings, George Campbell and Johnny Hale. Doc Cummings felt that Manning was trying to even the score for Campbell and Hale.

Cummings made the mistake of confronting Jim Manning in his own saloon. There was shooting, and Doc Cummings staggered into the street, shot twice in the chest, and there he died. With Cummings' death, the Mannings had evened the score.

El Paso was still waiting for the bloody continuation of the feud.

"With Doc Cummings dead," the bartender said, finishing up his story, "the marshal lost his only friend, and his only back up. He's now alone in his fight against the Mannings."

"What about a deputy?" asked Clint.

The man shook his head. "Ain't nobody willin' to pin on a deputy's badge for him."

"Why's that?"

"Lots of folks hereabouts side with the Mannings," the man explained. "Them that don't—

well, they don't want to go up against the Mannings."

"I see," Clint said.

At that moment the bat-wing doors of the saloon
entrance swung inward and admitted the man in
question, Marshal Dallas Stoudenmire.

SIX

As Stoudenmire approached the bar the bartender moved away to draw a beer. Obviously he knew what the marshal drank. He also had a nervous look on his face, as if he were afraid Stoudenmire would instinctively know that he'd been talking about Doc Cummings.

"I came to buy you that drink, Mr. Adams," Stoudenmire said.

"Clint, my name is Clint."

"Finish that up," Stoudenmire said, indicating the near-empty beer mug in Clint's hand, "and I'll buy you another." He looked at the bartender. "Dave, bring him another."

Dave nodded and put a fresh beer in front of each of them.

"Let's take these to a table," Stoudenmire said. "I have something to talk to you about."

"Okay," Clint said.

As they moved away from the bar Clint threw the bartender a look that told him not to worry, their secret was safe with him. Dave didn't look convinced.

The two men carried their beers to a table against the wall opposite the bar. As they sat down Clint asked, "What's on your mind, Marshal?"

"Your reason for being here," Stoudenmire answered.

"I thought I told you that."

"Yes," the lawman said. "You said you came here because you'd never been here before."

"That's right."

Stoudenmire leaned forward as he asked, "Is it that simple?"

"Marshal Stoudenmire," Clint said, because he didn't like word games, "why don't you just tell me why you think I'm here?"

"I don't think anything, Mr. Adams," Stoudenmire said, sitting back in his chair. "I am wondering something, though."

"Okay," Clint was willing to settle for that. "What's that?"

"I'm wondering if you've been hired by the Mannings." Stoudenmire stated.

"To do what?"

Stoudenmire frowned. "Why do you think the Mannings would hire somebody like you?" he asked.

"Somebody like me?" Clint asked, as if he wasn't sure what that meant. Actually, he knew exactly what the Marshal meant. "Oh, you mean somebody with the reputation of a mad dog killer?"

"Mr. Adams—"

"Somebody whose gun is for hire?" Clint asked. "Is that what you mean?"

"Adams—"

"Marshal," Clint said, "I've told you why I'm here. Now if you want to question me about it, you're going to have to be *very* specific."

"Very well," Stoudenmire said. "Did the Mannings hire you to kill me?"

"I don't hire out to kill people, Marshal," Clint said coldly. "I never have, and I'm sure as hell too old to start now."

Stoudenmire stared at Clint for a few moments, then said, "You know what?"

"No." Clint's tone was still cold. "What?"

"I believe you."

"Big deal."

Stoudenmire heaved a sigh. He suddenly looked very tired.

"Sorry, Adams, but I had to ask."

"Why?"

"Why did I have to ask?"

"No," Clint said, "I know the answer to that. Why do you believe me?"

"Because I do know your reputation."

"Okay," Clint said. "Then why *did* you feel you had to ask?"

"Because I wanted to see your eyes when you answered me."

"Well," Clint said, "I'm glad we have that settled, then."

"So am I," Stoudenmire agreed, then added with a wry grin, "Clint."

"So where do we go from here?" asked Clint.

"Just drink your beer," Stoudenmire said. "We're just having a friendly beer."

Clint sipped his beer, but he had the distinct feeling that Stoudenmire was not yet finished asking all his questions.

Behind the bar Dave watched the two men, trying to decide if they were friends, or if they had really just met, like the stranger said. The last thing he needed was for Stoudenmire to know he'd been talking about Doc Cummings.

Jesus, but he had a big mouth, he thought. Maybe that's what made him such a good bartender, but one of these days he just knew it was gonna get him killed.

SEVEN

"Are you sure about this, Sam?" John Manning asked Sam Jones.

"Yes, sir," Sam said. "I'm real sure."

John looked at Jim, who nodded. He thought the boy was telling the truth. He also thought that he was trying to score some points with his bosses, but Sam was smart enough to know not to lie to do that. He'd come across a piece of information and knew enough to use it to his advantage. It wasn't a bad thing to have somebody like that working for you.

"All right, Sam," John said. "We appreciate the information. Thank you."

"Sure, Mr. Manning," Sam said, backing towards the door, "sure."

He was almost out the door when Jim said, "Oh, and Sam?"

"Yes, sir?"

"You just got yourself a raise."

Sam smiled broadly. He said effusively, "Thank you, sir!"

Jim looked up at John as the door closed. "A *small* raise," he added.

John smiled and nodded. "Don't worry, he earned it. You want a brandy?" he asked his brother.

"Yes."

John poured two brandies and handed his younger brother one. There was only a year separating the two men, but as brothers usually are, they were acutely aware of who was the elder and who was the younger.

"What do you think?" John asked. "Is this fella really the Gunsmith?"

"I think we should find out."

"And if he is?"

"Then we need to know if he's just passing through," Jim replied, "or if he's here at Marshal Dallas Stoudenmire's request."

"And if he's just passing through?"

"Maybe," Jim said, "we can persuade him to stay a while."

"And if he's here to help Stoudenmire?" John pursued the matter further.

Jim looked up at his brother and raised his glass to him. "Then I guess we'll just have to kill ourselves a Gunsmith."

"You think that's smart, Jim?" John asked.

"John," Jim answered patiently, "I wouldn't suggest it if I didn't think it was smart."

"Well, maybe one of us should talk to him first."

"Well, then, you talk to him," Jim said. "You

have a way with strangers, John . . . and you're a much better talker than I am."

"Okay," John agreed. "But maybe we should hedge our bet first."

Jim looked at his brother. "How do you mean?"

John sipped some brandy before answering. "Well, if there's even the slightest chance that we're gonna have to . . . kill him, I'm thinking maybe we should bring somebody of our own in now."

"Like who?"

"Somebody with a rep," answered John. "Somebody good with a gun, and somebody who would like the idea of killing Clint Adams, the Gunsmith."

"I see what you mean," Jim said, scratching his chin. "Why wait to find out what he's here for before we bring in someone of our own? This way, we'll be ready for him, either way."

John nodded.

"Let's talk to Frank and Will," Jim suggested. "See what they have to say. They might be able to recommend someone."

"And Doc?" John asked.

Jim thought a moment, then frowned and shook his head slowly. "No," he said. "I don't think there's any reason to involve our older brother in this."

George Felix "Doc" Manning was the eldest of the Manning brothers, and the least involved in their somewhat dubious businesses.

"Frank would probably be the best one to talk

to," John went on. "After all, his place caters to
that . . . type of customer."

Jim smiled. Frank's Place was a little rougher
around the edges than the Coliseum, and did cater
to a whole different clientele. "So which one of us
talks to him?" he asked. "You or me?"

Neither one of them particularly liked going to
that part of town. Their brother Frank had less
refined tastes than either of them in everything—
women, whiskey—and friends.

John looked at Jim and then set down his empty brandy snifter. "I'll talk to Frank," he said.
"Why don't you talk to Will? We'll meet back here
later."

"Okay," Jim stood up. "Let's get it done, then."

EIGHT

When Dallas Stoudenmire finally spoke again Clint was not surprised by the question.

"When was the last time you wore a badge?" the marshal asked.

"A long time ago," Clint said. "I've had the opportunity since then, but . . ." He shook his head. "When I stopped wearing one it was for a reason, and the reason hasn't changed."

"What was the reason?" Stoudenmire asked. He added, "I mean, if I can ask."

Clint studied the man for a few moments, wondering if he should even get into this, and then decided, why the hell not?

"When you put a badge on your chest," Clint said, "everybody else around you absolves themselves of responsibility, for their own safety, for the safety of the town. It all becomes *your* job."

"But you know that when you take the job," Stoudenmire reasoned.

38

"Yes," Clint replied, "and no. Have you been a lawman before this?"

"Yes."

"Then you know how difficult it is to get a posse together," Clint said. "See, that's what they pay you for, to chase down bank robbers and all kinds of troublemakers. Why should *they* have to ride with you, and risk *their* lives when they're not being paid?"

Stoudenmire studied Clint for a few moments. "You've had some bad experiences," he said.

"Oh, I've had plenty of bad experiences," Clint agreed, "and most of them were while I was wearing a badge."

Stoudenmire said, "I guess that means I shouldn't even ask."

"You can always ask, Marshal," Clint said.

"Don't you think that *some*one has to wear the badge, though?" Stoudenmire asked. "Someone has to be there to . . . to help the people who *can't* help themselves?"

Clint leaned forward. "I can do that, Dallas. Hell, I *do* do that. I get into more scrapes trying to help people who need it, and I do it without wearing a badge, without getting paid for it."

Stoudenmire frowned.

"Also," Clint added, "I help people who truly can't help themselves, and not those who just won't."

Stoudenmire thought that over before answering in a thoughtful tone. "It does sound more . . . noble, the way you do it," he said, slowly.

"No," Clint said, sitting back in his chair, "it's not noble. And if I keep doing it, one of these days it's going to get me killed."

"You ever figure on dying some other way than from a bullet?" Stoudenmire asked.

"No," Clint replied. "I truly don't. I guess that's why I'll just keep on doing what I'm doing."

"Whatever the reasons," said Stoudenmire, "we seem to do the same things for people."

"I guess so," Clint agreed. "Tell me, why don't you have any deputies?"

Now Stoudenmire sat back in his chair and spread his arms wide. "It's this place," he said, and Clint knew he didn't mean the Top Dollar Saloon. "El Paso. You can't swing a dead cat by the tail in this town without hitting someone who's wanted on one side of the border or the other. The only ones who aren't wanted aren't willing, or aren't fit, to wear a badge."

"Why not bring someone in?" Clint asked.

"Who?"

"A friend?"

As he said it Clint wondered if Dallas Stoudenmire *had* any such friends, the kind you could call on for help like that. Clint knew that was the one thing he did have in this world—back up. If he needed someone to watch his back he could call on Bat Masterson, Wyatt Earp, Buckskin Frank Leslie, Ron Diamond, Fred Hammer, any number of men he knew who were good with a gun and could be trusted with his life.

"I don't think I have a friend I'd do that to," the

marshal said. "This place *is* a hellhole. Maybe not as bad as when I took it over, but as long as the Mannings are here, it won't change."

"The Mannings," Clint said. "Tell me something, Dallas . . . and tell me to mind my own business if you want to . . . but this thing with the Mannings, is it more . . . personal than anything else?"

Stoudenmire frowned as he thought the question over. "It is personal," he finally answered. "I can't deny that. But it didn't start out that way. When I got here I realized immediately that they were a big reason why this town is the way it is. I made them my number one priority, and when *they* decided to make the fight personal, I decided not to back down. Maybe that was wrong, but now I guess it's business *and* personal."

"Well," Clint replied, "you have to do what's right for you."

"That's what I've always done," Stoudemire stood up. "Right now I have to go and take my rounds. Thanks for the talk."

"Sure," Clint said. "Thanks for the beer."

Stoudenmire nodded, turned and left the saloon. Clint still had some beer left in his mug, so he took his time finishing it.

NINE

Elaine Mills's curiosity was aroused.

It started when she saw the good-looking stranger talking to the Coliseum's bartender, Sam Jones. Then, when Sam had sent her looking for their bosses because he had something interesting he wanted to tell them, that made it even stronger.

When she saw Sam Jones come out of the Mannings' office, she waited until he had taken his place behind the bar again and then approached. This time when she leaned her elbows on the bar and bent forward, she saw Sam's eyes go right down the front of her dress.

"So?"

"So what?" he asked, with a smile.

"Did Jim and John find what you had to say interesting?"

"Jim and John?" he asked.

"Well, what do you call them?"

"The same thing you do," he retorted. "'Boss.'"

"Okay," she said, "what did our bosses think of what you had to tell them?"

"They liked it," the young bartender said. "They found it very interesting."

"And how interesting is *very* interesting?"

Sam leaned closer to Elaine. "They liked it enough to give me a raise."

"A raise?" she said. "Well, I'm impressed."

"A big raise," he added.

"Oooh . . ." Elaine said, rolling her eyes.

"Are you impressed enough to come to my room tonight?" he asked, touching her arm with his forefinger. Sam had been trying to get her into his bed since he first started working at the Coliseum a couple of months earlier. So far, he hadn't been successful—and that wasn't about to change tonight.

"Not tonight, Sam," Elaine straightened up, taking her breasts out of his line of sight.

"When, then?"

"Oh, I don't know," she replied. "How would you like to tell me what you told the bosses?"

Sam frowned. "I don't think so, Elaine. I don't think *they'd* like that."

"My," she said, "this is a mystery, isn't it?"

"And I want to keep my job," Sam responded, "so it's gonna stay that way."

"You mean," she teased, "there's nothing I could do to change your mind?"

He shrugged sadly and went off to tend bar at the other end.

It may have been a mystery, Elaine thought, but it was one she was going to solve. . . .

Later, when she saw both Jim and John Manning come out of their office and leave the building, Elaine toyed with the idea of following them. But, of course, that would have been dangerous.

It was pretty obvious that whatever Sam Jones had told them that they had found so interesting had something to do with that stranger Sam had been talking to. So what she had to do now was find out who the stranger was, and maybe even talk to him.

She decided to wait and see if he would come back to the Coliseum that night. If not, then she would try to find out the next day where he was staying.

If Elaine Mills had one failing that she would admit to, it was her curiosity. It was something that, at twenty-five, she'd had to deal with all of her life. When her curiosity was awakened, like it was now, there was nothing she could do but satisfy it.

TEN

Clint Adams did not go back to the Coliseum that night. When he left the Top Dollar he decided to check out some of the other places in town.

He walked around and judged many of them by their appearance. Of course, in that regard they all paled in comparison to the Coliseum. But at the far end of town he found one that he thought was interesting and decided to go in. To get to the door he'd had to virtually fight through his weight in street whores, who were trying to convince him that there was more to interest him in their cribs than anywhere else.

The establishment that he finally decided to go into was called Frank's Saloon.

In the back of Frank's Saloon, in Frank Manning's office, he was sitting behind his desk, talking to his brother John.

"The Gunsmith, huh?" Frank said. "You and Jim think he's here to help Stoudenmire?"

45

"We don't know," John replied. "Maybe."

"What are you gonna do?"

"I'll talk to him some," John said, "see if I can figure out why he's here. Meanwhile, we were thinking that we might have to import some talent."

"Somebody good with a gun, who would welcome the chance to go up against the Gunsmith and his rep?" Frank inquired.

"Right."

Frank shook his head. "Where do you expect to find somebody that dumb?"

"Okay, then," John said, "somebody who'll do it for money."

Frank nodded. "Now *that* I can help you with."

To Clint, Frank's Saloon was more what a saloon should look like. No leather, no crystal, a scarred and pitted bar. One bartender who was fat, two girls who looked weary, and a bunch of dusty, cheaply dressed cowboys out to have a good time.

He went to the bar and ordered a beer. When it came it was ice cold.

"Just out of curiosity," Clint asked the fat bartender, "and because I'm a stranger in town, who owns this place?"

"Frank Manning owns it."

"Manning?" Clint replied. "Is he related to the Mannings who own the Coliseum?"

"They're brothers," the bartender said. "All the Mannings are brothers."

"And what about—"

"And," the bartender cut Clint off, "it ain't healthy to ask questions about any of them."

Clint eyed the bartender for a moment. "I'll keep that in mind."

"You do that," the barman said.

When Clint turned to look the room over, the bartender walked to the other end of the bar and said something to a tall, slender man with a pockmarked face. The man nodded, walked to the back of the room and knocked on a door.

Both John and Frank Manning looked up as Gabe Wager entered the room.

"What is it, Gabe?" Frank asked.

"Ted sent me in to tell you there's a stranger at the bar askin' questions about you."

"About me?" Frank asked.

"About all of the Mannings," Wager answered.

John and Frank exchanged a glance, then both stood up and walked to the door. Frank cracked it so they could look out.

"Which one?" he asked Wager.

"Far end of the bar, nearer the window, Boss," Wager said.

"I see 'im," Frank said.

"So do I," John said.

"Is that him?" Frank asked.

"I don't know," his older brother answered. "I've never seen him before."

"You want me to brace him, Boss?" Wager asked Frank Manning.

Frank turned his head and looked at his man.

He was tempted to say yeah, sure, go ahead and brace the Gunsmith, Gabe. Instead he answered, "I don't think so, Gabe. I ain't quite ready to replace you yet."

"Replace me?" Wager responded with disdain. "What are you sayin', that I can't handle some saddle tramp—?"

"If we're right," John said to Wager, "that's not just some saddle tramp out there."

"Well, if it ain't," Wager asked, "then who is it?"

"Clint Adams," John Manning said.

"The Gunsmith," Frank Manning added.

"The Gunsmith?" Gabe Wager asked, in surprise.

Frank grinned. "Still wanna go and brace him, Gabe?"

Gabe didn't answer. Frank turned his attention to his brother. "Well, whataya say, brother?"

John frowned. "What do I say to what?"

"You said you wanted to talk to him," Frank answered. "No time like the present, I say."

"We don't even know if it's him," John said.

"There's only one way to find out." Frank looked at Gabe Wager.

"What?"

"Go on out and brace him, Gabe," Frank said. "If he kills you, we'll know he's the Gunsmith."

Wager stared at his employer for a long moment and started to sweat profusely. A drop rolled from between his eyes, down his nose and then dripped off. "That ain't funny, Boss," he said, finally.

Frank patted his man on the arm. "I was just funnin' with you, Gabe. No, me and John, we'll just go out and ask him straight out if he's Clint Adams."

"We will?" John asked, looking dubious.

"Yeah," Frank said, swinging the door wide open, "we will."

ELEVEN

Clint had noticed the bartender's eyes go to the back of the room. He turned and followed the fat man's line of vision and saw the door to the office open. Three men were coming out of that room; he watched as one of them broke off and the other two approached the bar. It took a moment for him to realize that they were also approaching him.

He met the eyes of the first man, the taller and younger one. The two men certainly looked enough alike to be brothers. Clint had a feeling that he was facing two of the Manning brothers.

"My name's Frank Manning," the first man said. He smiled broadly and offered his hand.

"Ah," Clint said, shaking the man's hand, "the Frank who owns this place?"

"That's right," Frank Manning replied. He released Clint's hand and indicated the man standing behind him. "This is my brother John."

John stepped forward and offered his hand, which Clint also shook. However, John was not wearing a smile anywhere near as friendly as his brother's. He wore a sort of humorless grin, and his eyes were studying Clint in frank appraisal.

"You own the Coliseum," Clint said to John.

John's eyes flicked to Frank and then he said, "Ah, that's right, my brother Jim and I do."

"I was over there earlier," Clint remarked. "It's quite a place."

"Thanks," John Manning said, still wary. "We like to think so."

"You seem to know a lot about what we own, Mr. . . ." Frank said.

"Adams," Clint said, "Clint Adams."

"Mr. Adams," Frank said. "You seem to know a little bit about us. How is that?"

"Well, it's not that difficult, is it?" Clint answered. "I mean, ever since I got to town all I hear is that the Mannings own almost everything."

Frank laughed, and John looked even more uncomfortable than before. "That's a slight exaggeration," Frank said, "but my family does have quite a few, uh, business interests in El Paso."

" 'Quite a few' strikes me as something of an understatement," replied Clint.

"You, uh, just ride into town today, Mr. Adams?" Frank asked, ignoring Clint's last remark.

"That's right. That's why I'm wondering what I've done to merit this kind of attention—two

Manning brothers at one time."

"Oh," Frank replied, waving a hand and looking at his brother John for a moment, "we just like to welcome strangers into town. We, uh, like to urge them to spend money in our places."

"Uh-huh," Clint said. "So it's just good business, right?"

"That's right," Frank agreed. "Good business. I see you're almost finished with your beer. Can we buy you another one?"

Clint looked down at the small amount of beer left in his mug. "I don't think so," he said. "I think I'll just finish this and turn in."

"Already?" asked Frank. "The night's young. Don't we have anything here to interest you? Ladies, games, some fine whiskey—"

"It's not that—"

"Maybe John has something you'll like at his place, huh?" Frank offered. "He could walk over there with you, introduce you around? Whataya say, John?"

"Sure," John said. "I'd like to show you our place proper, Mr. Adams."

"See," Frank said. "And John means it, Mr. Adams. He's real proud of the Coliseum."

"I'm sure he is," Clint replied, "but I rode all day, and I'm kind of beat."

"Well . . . maybe tomorrow, then?" Frank said. "We'll leave you with an open invitation. Whenever you're ready. I mean, we wouldn't want to interfere in whatever business brought you to El Paso."

Clint drained his mug and put it down easily on the bartop. They were asking him what he was doing in town without actually asking him. He decided not to give them any kind of an answer.

"Sure," he said, agreeably, "maybe tomorrow. Good night, gentlemen."

"Good night," Frank said. Behind him, John simply nodded.

Just outside the place Clint stopped and waited to see if anyone was going to come out behind him. They might decide to send someone to try to take him out or simply to follow him. When no one came out at all he shrugged and started down the street towards his hotel. Apparently the Mannings weren't ready to make any kind of move on him, and that suited him just fine. He hadn't come to El Paso looking for trouble anyway, had he?

But then, when had he ever had to go *looking* for trouble?

As Clint started for the door John nudged his brother's elbow. "Nice job," John said to Frank, sarcastically. "We didn't find out a thing."

Frank turned his head and stared at his brother over his shoulder. "I didn't notice you helping all that much, Brother," he said.

"Hey," John protested, spreading his arms, "your place, you do the talking."

"Well," Frank said, turning around to face his older, better-dressed brother, "maybe tomorrow night he'll be in your place, and you can do all the talking."

John frowned at that. "What do you think we should do, Frank?"

"There's no point in making a move against him yet, John," Frank answered. "Hell, he hasn't *done* anything but talk and drink. Let's just wait a little longer and see what Mr. Adams has in mind for his visit to El Paso."

"I agree," said John. "Meanwhile, line somebody up, will you? Let's be ready for when we *do* have to make a move."

TWELVE

Clint walked on back to his hotel, thinking about the two Manning brothers he had just met. Why had they been so interested in him? He had almost reached his hotel when he realized the answer. He'd been in three saloons that day—the Top Dollar, the Coliseum, and Frank's Saloon—and in all three he had asked questions about the Mannings. Obviously, the word had gotten around that a stranger was asking questions, and this was their attempt to find out who he was and what he wanted.

Well, he certainly hadn't made it easy on them, so they would undoubtedly be trying again tomorrow. Tonight had been—oh, some entertainment for him, to watch them trying to get his name from him. Tomorrow, he wasn't sure he'd want to make it so hard on the Mannings. They might not take it too kindly a second time.

On the other hand if they had just asked him what he was doing in town he probably would have told them. It was the way they were treating him that had annoyed him, like he'd respond to the smiles and offers of free drinks by just running off at the mouth.

When he reached his hotel he saw the outline of a man standing on the boardwalk right in front. He caught a glint of moonlight off of metal, and knew that it was Marshal Dallas Stoudenmire.

"Turning in early?" the lawman asked. He stepped out of the shadows and into the moonlight.

"I thought I would, yeah," Clint said. "I was in the saddle most of the day."

"That'll take it out of you, all right," Stoudenmire agreed.

"It sure will."

"Did you see any of the town today?"

"As a matter of fact," Clint said, "I saw the Coliseum today."

Stoudenmire looked interested. "Impressed?"

"Oh, yeah," Clint nodded. "It's quite an establishment."

"It's an impressive place, all right," said Stoudenmire. "What else did you see?"

"Frank's Saloon."

"Ah," Stoudenmire said, "another Manning place. Were you checking them out, or is it just a coincidence that you found yourself at two Manning places?"

"According to what I've heard," Clint said, actually paraphrasing the marshal himself, "you can't swing a dead cat in this town without hitting something the Mannings own."

"That's true."

"So I guess you could call it a coincidence," Clint said, then added, "if you wanted to."

The marshal studied Clint for a few moments, but apparently decided not to ask anything right out.

"You might be interested to know," Clint offered, "that two of them approached me."

"Oh?" Stoudenmire replied. He was obviously very much interested. "Which two?"

"Frank and John."

"Who did the talking?"

"Frank."

"Were you in Frank's place, at the time?"

"Yes."

Stoudenmire put his hand to his long jaw and stroked it thoughtfully. "Might be they knew who you were," he said. "If that was the case, they might also think that I sent for you."

"Well, I didn't keep it a secret who I was," Clint said. "We simply introduced ourselves. What they were doing was *trying* to find out what I was doing in town," Clint explained.

"And you didn't tell them?"

"No."

"Why not?"

Clint shrugged. "They never came right out and asked."

"Well . . . they're curious about you, anyway," the marshal said. "That much is certain. Whether they know who you are or not, you're a stranger.

They'll want to make sure they know why you're here—if there is some particular reason."

"I told you the reason," Clint replied. "I'm under no obligation to tell them."

"You don't want to make enemies of the Manning brothers, Clint," Stoudenmire said. "Not in this town, anyway."

"Thanks for the warning. I'll keep it in mind, Dallas," answered Clint. "Good night."

" 'Night."

Clint started into the hotel, then stopped in the entrance and turned.

"Dallas?"

"Yeah?"

"What are you doing here, tonight? Looking for me?"

"Just wanted to make sure you got back to your hotel safely," Stoudenmire replied. "After all, that *is* my job, isn't it?"

"I suppose so," Clint said. "Good night."

He went inside and up to his room, wondering who he should watch out for more—the Mannings or Dallas Stoudenmire.

Dallas Stoudenmire walked back to his office, thinking about the Manning brothers and about Clint Adams. Now that the Mannings had found out that Clint Adams—the Gunsmith—was in town they'd want to know why. They'd want to know if he was just passing through, or if Stoudenmire had sent for him. Once they were satisfied that the marshal had not sent for the

Gunsmith, they might try to recruit Clint Adams themselves.

Stoudenmire considered that he had three options open to him. One, he *could* try to recruit Adams, even without getting him to wear a badge; two, he could wait and see if the Mannings managed to recruit him; or three, he could run Adams out of town—or, at least, ask the man to leave.

The second and third options figured to have him facing off with the Gunsmith. While he wouldn't hesitate to do so if his job called for it, it wasn't something he was looking forward to.

He had enough trouble with the Mannings. He didn't need to add a big gun rep to his problems.

THIRTEEN

"We can't let Clint Adams change our plans," Jim Manning warned his brothers, John and Frank. "Dallas Stoudenmire has to go."

"We're agreed on that, Jim," Frank said. "But first we have to find out what Adams is doing here."

"Did you find out from Jones what Adams looks like?" John asked Jim.

"Yeah," Jim answered. "He matches the description of the man you and John said you talked to last night at your place."

"Me and John?" Frank said, sarcastically.

"I told you," John snapped. "It was your place so I let you do the talking."

"Sure," Frank said. "Right."

"Never mind who did the talking," Jim said from behind his desk. He looked at his brothers disapprovingly. "We're not gonna get anywhere if we fight among ourselves."

"We're not fighting," Frank protested. "I'm just

teasing my big brother, is all."

"Well, cut it out," Jim ordered.

Frank gave Jim a quick look. He seemed about to argue but then let it drop. "Okay," he said, instead. "So how are we going to play it today?"

"One of us will talk to Adams point blank and find out why he's here," said Jim. "If he's gonna back Stoudenmire we need to know, and know fast."

"Either way," Frank said, "I've sent for someone to come and help us. If we need to handle Adams, my man will be here. If Adams is out of it, we'll just use my man for Stoudenmire, along with the others."

"Okay," Jim agreed. "When will he get here?"

"Later today," Frank answered, "maybe early tomorrow. He'll be here for sure tomorrow."

"When do we hit Stoudenmire?" asked John.

"I want Stoudenmire gone by the end of the week," Jim stated. "This has gone on long enough, as it is. With the marshal gone, our business will pick up again. He's been cuttin' into our profits long enough."

"Okay," John said. "Who talks to him?"

"I think John should do it," Frank suggested, with a smirk on his face.

"Listen, Frank—" John argued, lifting his butt off the edge of Jim's desk.

"Settle down," Jim said, harshly. "I'll talk to Adams myself."

"When?" Frank asked.

"Today," he answered, "as soon as I can."

"You want us to back you up?"

"No," said Jim. "I don't want it to look like we're ganging up on him. I'll talk to him alone."

"Better take a gun," John said.

Jim gave his older brother a disparaging look. "What for? If he wants to kill me, do you think I can outdo him with a gun?"

"Well—," John said.

"Having a gun might get *me* killed," Jim went on. "No, I'll go and see him unarmed. I won't have anything to fear from him."

"Not this time, anyway," Frank said.

"Maybe you should take somebody with you, anyway," John suggested. "Just to play it safe."

"When have we ever played anything safe, John?" Jim asked. "No, it might even impress him that I'm facing him alone and unarmed. We don't want him thinking that *any* Manning is afraid of him. He has to know that we hold this town in an iron fist."

"Yeah," Frank said, "except for Marshal Dallas Stoudenmire."

Jim turned to Frank. "That may be so, but we'll be taking care of that little problem soon enough, won't we?"

"You bet we will," Frank agreed.

John, less of a man of action than his two brothers, wasn't so sure.

"What are you gonna do today?" John asked Jim. "Wait until Adams comes into the Coliseum?"

"No," Jim answered. "I'll find him and talk to

him as soon as possible."

"And how are you gonna do that?" asked John.

"How do we do anything?" Frank replied to John's question. "Put the word out on the street."

"Right," Jim said. "Frank?"

"I'll handle it, Jim," Frank said, and left the office.

"What the hell is the matter with you?" Jim demanded of John after their brother had left.

"What do you mean?"

"You and Frank are goin' at each other," Jim answered. "I want to know why."

John stood up, shuffled his feet like a kid and shrugged. "I don't do things the way you two do, Jim," he said, finally.

"We get results, John," Jim said. "You and I know we do things differently. You run the Coliseum, and I run everything else. We've never had a problem with that before. Do we now?"

"No. . . ."

"Don't let Frank get to you, John," Jim said. "We have to work together to get rid of Stoudenmire."

John didn't reply immediately.

"John?"

"I'm not so sure about killing Stoudenmire, Jim," John finally answered. "Killing a lawman might bring a lot of heat down on us."

"John," said Jim, "nobody cares about El Paso. Nobody cares about border towns. Everybody knows they're wide open. It's just do-gooders like Stoudenmire who are trying to make trouble for the rest of us."

"I know—"

"We have to get rid of him," Jim said. "We know we can't run him out, so there's only one way to do it. Right?"

"I guess—"

"We've *talked* about this, John," Jim said, slamming his hand down on the desk for emphasis. "It has to be done. There's no way around it—unless you want *us* to leave El Paso?"

"No," John replied, "no, I don't want that. We have too much invested here."

"That's right," Jim said, "we do. John, leave Clint Adams and Dallas Stoudenmire to me. You just keep this place in booze, dealers and girls. Okay?"

"Sure," the older brother said, feeling very much like the younger, lesser brother. "Sure, Jim."

FOURTEEN

Clint awoke the next morning with Wynona
Jamison's avid mouth at work between his legs.

After he had left Marshal Stoudenmire in front
of the hotel the night before he'd gone up to his
room and found the lady waiting for him in his
bed. It was certainly not the first time this had
happened to him. Clint Adams was used to wom-
en liking him, and sometimes they came up to his
room to show him just how much.

He usually knew how to handle the situation.

"How did you get past the marshal?" he asked,
closing the door behind him.

She was sitting propped up by the pillows
behind her. The sheet was down around her
waist, and she made no attempt to cover her
full, firm breasts. Hell, and why should she?
She was proud as hell of them, that much was
certain.

"I saw him in front of the hotel," she said, smiling. "Was he waiting for you?"

"He was."

"Are you in trouble with the law, Clint?" she asked. "Am I in the bed of a wanted man? A . . . what do you call them . . . desperado?"

He laughed. "No, I'm not a desperado," he said, "and I'm not wanted by the law."

"Well," she said, "maybe you ain't wanted by the law, Mr. Adams, but you *are* by me."

She tossed the sheet aside completely, so that she was completely naked. She was not a slender woman, and he saw her heavy thighs and hips, and the dark patch of hair at the apex of her thighs. She was a big, solid woman, and he felt himself responding not only to the sight of her but to the scent of her as well.

She smelled ready.

He shucked his clothing quickly and joined her on the bed. She grabbed for him and drew him to her, kissing him hotly, wetly. Her thighs opened and closed, pinning his erection between them. She was a strong woman as well as a sturdy one, and it was not without difficulty that he parted her thighs so he could enter her. It was almost like a wrestling match, but finally he slid into her and she gasped as he pierced her deeply.

"Oh, God. . . ." she moaned and closed her powerful legs around his waist.

He drove into her then, fiercely, powerfully, and she lifted her hips to meet each of his thrusts with one of her own. She was a loud woman during sex, moaning and crying out, clutching at him, clawing at him, beating his buttocks with her heels and then finally tightening around him, making him feel as if he'd never escape from her—and then she literally *yanked* his orgasm from him and cried out as she came, as well.

Now, as the morning sunlight came streaming in through the window, Wynona used her tongue to wake him, licking him until he was fully erect and moaning. He reached for her but before he could take hold of her, her mouth swooped down on him, taking him inside. He lifted his hips as she began to suckle him, moaning, a long, drawn out humming sound that excited him. Suddenly he was exploding and bucking and, strong woman that she was, she was staying with him, continuing to suck until she had drained him completely. . . .

He watched with pleasure as she dressed.

"Look at me," Wynona said with a shy expression. "I been in bed with you all night, we done all sorts of things to each other, but you're making me shy just by watching me dress."

"I like watching women dress."

"And I bet you've watched a lot of them haven't you?" she asked.

"A few."

"Yeah," she said, "more than a few, I'd wager, Clint Adams."

He didn't comment.

"You comin' in for breakfast?"

"Is there a better place in town to eat?" he asked.

"Yes."

"Well," Clint said, "I'll come by you, anyway. Have the coffee ready."

"It'll be ready," she replied, "and hot, and black, just the way you like it."

Wynona went to the bed, leaned over and kissed him. She made liberal use of her tongue, moaning and wetting him thoroughly. "Give me an hour," she said.

He considered asking her where her husband thought she was all night but then decided against it. Why get that involved? After all he'd only had her physically, and he wasn't all that concerned with having her any other way. He knew she felt the same way, too. This had been a purely physical thing, and there was no guarantee that it would ever happen again.

As she went out the door Clint thought that suited him. She'd been a wonderful bed partner and he'd welcome her back if she came, but he wouldn't go after her.

Except in an hour, for breakfast.

FIFTEEN

Clint went back to the San Antonio Street cafe for breakfast, as promised, and Wynona had the coffee hot and waiting for him. She came out of the kitchen with his food, served it with a smile and went off to serve other customers. She gave them all as much or as little attention as she gave him. No one who saw them that morning would know that they had spent the night together, which was probably the way Wynona wanted it. It was fine with him, too.

Clint Adams didn't know when he walked into the cafe that he had been spotted from across the street, and that the word had gotten back to the Manning brothers even before he'd been served his food.

Jim Manning had decided to have a look at Clint Adams himself, so when he heard where Clint was having breakfast he left his office and started over there.

69

• • •

What the Mannings didn't know was that Dallas Stoudenmire knew what was going on. He had heard the word on the street, as well, and he knew the exact moment when Jim Manning left the Coliseum and walked over to San Antonio Street.

Clint was putting his second forkful of eggs into his mouth when a man entered the small cafe and Clint saw Wynona stop short and stare. Clint turned and looked to see what—or who—it was that she found so interesting.

He immediately noticed the resemblance between this man and the two Manning brothers he had met the night before. When Wynona spoke to him, it confirmed what he already had guessed.

"Mr. Manning." Her tone was one of complete surprise, and nervousness. Obviously the Mannings did not often have breakfast in her cafe.

He looked at her and said, "Hello, Miss."

"What can I get you, Mr. Manning?" she asked, wiping her hands on her apron. There was nothing on her hands, she was just extremely nervous.

"I'm looking for someone," Manning replied.

"Excuse me," Clint said to Wynona.

"Yes?"

"I think Mr. Manning will be joining me for breakfast," he said.

Jim Manning looked at Clint, and then back to the woman. "Just coffee."

"Could you bring another cup, please?" Clint asked. "And more coffee?"

"Oh . . . of course," she said. "Right away."

Clint looked at Manning and indicated the chair across from him.

"That's very kind of you," Manning said.

As the man sat Clint said, "And you'd be . . ."

"James Manning," the other man answered. "Or Jim, if you prefer. And you *are* Clint Adams, aren't you?"

"That's right."

"You talked to my brothers last night."

"I did."

"They suspected who you were," Manning explained, "but they didn't know for sure until you told them. You, uh, didn't tell them why you were in town, though. They were interested."

"Really? Actually," said Clint, "they never asked."

"I see," Jim Manning responded. "Well, I can understand—I mean, I guess a man of your reputation can't go around volunteering his plans, can he?"

"I guess not."

The woman came back with a full pot of coffee and an empty cup. "Can I pour?" she asked.

"Please," Manning said.

She poured their two cups full and put the pot down on the table. "Mr. Manning, can I get you something to eat?" she asked, anxiously.

Manning looked at Clint before answering, and
Clint shook his head just enough for the other
man to catch.

"No, thank you," Manning replied. "The coffee
will be fine."

"Well," she said, "you'll let me know if you
change your mind?"

"Of course," Manning said. "Thank you."

As she walked away Manning said to Clint,
"Thanks for the warning."

"The food is fair at best," said Clint. "Certainly
not what a man like you must be used to."

Manning took a sip from his cup. "Coffee's good,
though."

"Yes," Clint agreed. "So, tell me what's on your
mind, Mr. Manning."

"Jim, please," Manning said.

"Oh, I think I'll wait on the first name business
until we establish the ground rules."

Manning fixed Clint with a steady look, as if
trying to decide whether or not to be insulted.
"You're a cautious man, Mr. Adams."

"No more or less than you are, Mr. Manning,"
said Clint. "Of that I'm sure."

SIXTEEN

"I'll get right to it, then," Manning said. "My brothers and I are curious."

"About what?" asked Clint.

"About you," Manning said, "and what brings you to El Paso."

"Now that's funny."

"What is?"

"Well, when I got to town the marshal asked me exactly the same question."

"He did?"

"That's right."

"And did you tell him?"

"Sure I did," Clint said. "After all, he's the law in El Paso, isn't he? *He* had a right to ask."

Jim Manning looked at Clint for a few seconds, then sat back and nodded.

"I see," he said. "He had a right to ask, and I don't. Is that your point?"

"That's it exactly."

73

"Well," Manning said, "I think you have the wrong idea about who runs El Paso, Mr. Adams."

"Is that so?" Clint inquired. "Well, I'm sure you'll be only too glad to enlighten me, Mr. Manning."

"Without playing games?" asked Manning.

Clint nodded for Manning to continue. "I'd appreciate it if we could do this without playing games," he said.

"All right, then. Stoudenmire's days in this town are numbered, Mr. Adams," Manning said. "He has a lot of enemies."

"You and your brothers included?"

"It's no secret that my brothers and I, and the marshal, don't see eye to eye."

"So what are you telling me exactly, Mr. Manning?" Clint asked.

"I'm not telling you anything, Mr. Adams," Manning replied. "I'm asking you if you are in town to back Dallas Stoudenmire's play."

"That wasn't my intention when I came to town, no," Clint told him. "Not that it's any of your business—or your brothers'—but I'll tell you why I came to town, Manning. I'll tell you the same thing I told the marshal."

"Which was?"

Clint leaned forward slightly as he said, "I've never been here before."

Manning waited. When Clint didn't speak again he said, "That's it?"

"That's it."

Jim Manning frowned. "Did Stoudenmire buy that?"

"I don't know if he did or didn't," said Clint. "Why don't you ask him?"

Manning studied Clint for a few seconds, then pushed his chair back.

"Leaving already?" Clint asked him.

"Yes, but not without giving you some advice," Manning answered.

"I'm all ears."

"Leave town."

"Why?"

"Things are going to get ugly," Manning warned, "and I wouldn't want you to be tempted to take sides."

"Like the marshal's, you mean?" Clint asked. "I mean, he *is* all alone, isn't he? He could probably use some help, couldn't he?"

Manning stood up and shook his head, looking down at Clint.

"That's not the way you want to start thinking, Adams," Manning said. "Believe me."

Clint pointed at Manning with his knife. "See, this is why I wanted to wait before we started using first names. I think we've gotten off on the wrong foot, don't you?"

"Just take my advice, Adams," Manning repeated. "Leave town."

Clint pointed his knife at his plate. "I haven't finished my breakfast."

"Leave town," Manning said, "and live to eat a lot more breakfasts."

Clint frowned as Manning started for the door. He asked in a loud voice, "Does this mean I can't come into the Coliseum tonight?"

Manning left without replying.

SEVENTEEN

Just minutes after Jim Manning left the cafe Marshal Dallas Stoudenmire walked in.

Wynona Jamison came out of the kitchen and looked around, obviously searching for Jim Manning. She saw Stoudenmire, and once again she displayed surprise.

"Another cup?" she asked Clint.

"Please," he said.

Stoudenmire sat in the chair recently vacated by Manning.

"You watching me?" Clint asked.

"Watching *out* for you, is more like it," Stoudenmire responded. "The word on the street was that the Mannings were looking for you."

"Well, one of them found me."

"I know," Stoudenmire said. "Jim."

"You saw him leave?"

"I saw him come in," Stoudenmire replied.

"I was in no danger," Clint said. "He didn't have a gun."

"I'm sure he did that to keep *himself* out of danger," Stoudenmire said. "Did he know who you were when he came in?"

"Yeah, he did," said Clint.

"Did he try to hire you?"

"No," Clint answered. "He advised me to leave town right away."

"Why?"

Clint finished his last bite. "He said I'd live to eat more breakfasts."

Wynona came back at that point with the empty cup, and Clint told her that they would pour for themselves, this time.

"Sounds like a threat to me," Stoudenmire said after she'd left them alone.

"Oh, it definitely was," Clint agreed. "He also said that it wouldn't be healthy for me to stay around and choose sides."

"His or mine?"

"Well, not yours, anyway," Clint said. "He never did get around to admitting that he and his brothers were on the other side. He did say that you had a lot of enemies in town, though."

"I do," Stoudenmire admitted, rubbing his jaw, "but none worse than him and his brothers. I guess by not trying to hire you yet, he avoided admitting that he and his brothers want to kill me."

"He only said that you and them didn't see eye to eye."

"Well then, he told the truth, as far as he went. What do you intend to do?"

"That's a tough one," Clint answered. "I actually think I've seen all El Paso has to offer, but if I leave now the word will get out that the Manning brothers ran me out of town."

"Does that really matter to you?" asked Stoudenmire. "You don't strike me as the type of man who has something to prove."

"I don't," Clint said. "But if they spread the word that I can be scared out of town, I won't be able to go anywhere anymore."

Stoudenmire frowned. "I see your point. You'd be even more of a target than you are now."

"So I guess I'll be around at least a few more days," Clint finished.

"Well, let *me* give you some advice, then," the marshal said.

"Go ahead."

"Stay neutral," Stoudenmire said. "Don't pick a side—theirs *or* mine."

"You're totally alone in this, aren't you?" Clint asked him.

Stoudenmire shook his head. "Don't worry about that, Clint. Whatever happens is between me and the Mannings."

"And whoever they send after you," Clint said. "They won't do it themselves, you know. Those kind never do. They'll hire it done."

"I know they will," replied Stoudenmire. "They've tried it before."

"They'll keep trying until they find the right talent to do it," Clint said. "Why don't you just let them have El Paso, Dallas?"

"I guess for the same reason you won't leave town," Stoudenmire replied. "Where would I ever be able to wear a badge again if I did that?"

"And I can see *your* point," said Clint. He took out his money to pay the check.

Stoudenmire stood up. "Going back to your hotel?"

"I guess so," Clint said. "There won't be much to do until later."

"Like what?"

"Guess I'll pass the time playing poker," Clint said. "That is, if I can get a game up in the Top Dollar."

"Come on," Stoudenmire said, "I'll walk you back to your hotel."

"I don't need a bodyguard, Marshal."

"I know that," answered Stoudenmire. He paused, then added, "I'll walk you, anyway."

EIGHTEEN

"You think he's gonna leave?" Frank Manning asked his brother Jim.

Jim frowned and didn't answer right away. He was angry at himself.

"What's wrong?" Frank asked.

"I went about it wrong."

"Whataya mean?"

They were once again in Jim's office at the Coliseum, but this time John wasn't present.

"I tried pushing him."

"So? Why was that wrong?"

"Ah!" Jim said, striking out at the air as he gave vent to his anger. "A man like that won't push, Frank. All I did by threatening him was make sure he'd stay a while. All I did was make damn sure that we *are* gonna have to deal with him. It was stupid on my part."

"So? Why don't we just wait him out? Wait until he leaves?"

"No!" Jim slapped his palm down on his desk.

"I want to deal with Stoudenmire now!"

"All right, Jim, relax," Frank told his brother soothingly. "We'll take care of Stoudenmire, and if Adams gets in the way we'll take care of him, too. Just don't get yourself all worked up over it."

"You're right," Jim said, trying to relax. "You're right. I've got to relax. Get me a drink, will you, Frank?"

"A drink?" Frank said. "Uh, you want this brandy stuff you and John like so much?"

"No," said Jim. "Get me a whiskey."

"All right," Frank answered. "And I'll have one along with you."

Frank poured out two stiff drinks and handed his brother one. "Here's to the end of Dallas Stoudenmire's term as Marshal of El Paso," he said, raising his glass to his brother.

"I'll drink to that."

Frank put his empty glass down on his brother's desk. He had decided to bring up a subject they hadn't talked about for a while.

"Jim?"

"What?"

Frank hesitated, then went on. "We ought to do this ourselves, you know."

"No," Jim said, shaking his head. "We talked about this before, Frank."

"You used to be pretty good with a gun, Jim," Frank said, "and I can handle one."

"We're businessmen, Frank," Jim replied, "not gunmen. We've got the money to hire guns, and that's what we're gonna do."

"We've done that before, Jim," Frank reminded him, "and it didn't work."

"Sometimes it worked in the past."

"With Stoudenmire it didn't."

"Then we'll keep doing it until it *does* work," Jim said stubbornly.

"Jim—"

"Don't argue with me, Frank!"

Frank didn't like the sharp edge to his brother's tone. After all, they were brothers—equals. He didn't *work* for Jim.

"All right," Frank agreed, "all right, Jim, I won't argue with you. I'll just tell you something."

"What?"

"If it doesn't work this time, if the hired guns can't finish Stoudenmire this time, then I'm taking a hand next time," he said.

"Frank—"

"You can stay behind a desk with John, if you want," Frank told him, backing towards the door. "But if it don't get done this time, then *I'm* doin' it myself next time. I ain't arguin' with you, Jim, I'm just making you a promise—and I aim to keep it."

"Frank—," Jim called, but his brother turned and went out of the office, slamming the door hard behind him.

Here he was arguing with Frank, when earlier he had been bawling John out for the same thing. What the hell was going on? They *never* used to argue before.

Stoudenmire, he thought, that's what it was.

Ever since Stoudenmire came to town they had all been on edge, and now they were arguing among themselves.

Well fine, he thought, all the more reason why Stoudenmire had to be taken care of, and now!

Once outside the office, Frank stalked through the Coliseum and out the front door. He was fuming. He longed for the time when the Mannings handled their own problems themselves, without hiring guns. It was a waste of money. He'd meant what he'd said to Jim, and whether Jim or John or any of the others would help him or not, if this didn't work he was going to kill Stoudenmire himself!

NINETEEN

The next morning another stranger rode into town. He arrived at a particularly busy time of the day, and consequently his progress was watched by a lot of people—not all of whom were watching from the street.

During the night both Clint Adams and Dallas Stoudenmire, quite separately from each other, formed the same opinion. They each felt that since the Mannings could not be sure of Clint Adams' neutrality, or which side he would take, they would probably import some talent to set against Clint if the need arose. In both cases they decided that's what *they* would have done.

Consequently, they both found the newly arrived stranger very interesting.

Dallas Stoudenmire watched from the window of his office as the man rode into town. He got a clear look at the man's face as he rode by the office, and did not not recognize it. Still, he had a face in mind now, and went to his desk to go through his wanted posters. With a little luck, the man's face would show up on one, and he'd have an excuse to either lock him up, or run him out of town.

He didn't need to have to deal with another stranger's presence in town, wondering what he was doing here, who he was working for. Besides, the man had the look of a hard case. If there was paper on him it would give the marshal ample cause to ask him to leave town. He would just be doing his job.

Clint watched from a chair in front of the hotel as the stranger rode by. He didn't recognize the man, but he certainly recognized the type. The man never turned his head, but Clint was sure that he took in everything as he rode down El Paso Street.

Of course, the man could have been in El Paso for the same reason as Clint—or for his own reasons. He didn't *have* to be in town at the behest of the Mannings. If that were the case, he was simply unfortunate enough to be riding into a bad situation.

Come to think of it, the same could have been said for Clint himself.

Possibly the only person in town who saw the stranger ride into town and recognized him was

Frank Manning, since it was he who had sent for the man.

The other men they were going to send against Stoudenmire were already in place. It was the arrival of Clint Adams that had made employing *this* man necessary. Now that he had arrived in town, all the pieces were in place.

Frank left his place and went to tell his brother Jim that they could put their plan into action at any time now. Everything was set for the downfall of Marshal Dallas Stoudenmire.

Frank's early arrival at Jim's door had pulled Jim Manning from a warm bed and a willing woman, so he was annoyed when he finally came down to his office, fully dressed.

"Sorry to take you away from, uh, your comfortable bed, Jim," Frank said, "but I figured you'd want to know. He's here."

"Who's here?" Jim asked, irritably. He was still thinking about the woman. She'd been warm and willing, and goddamn but she was the wettest woman he'd ever had his fingers . . .

"My man," Frank said. "The man I sent for to take care of Adams."

"Your man," Jim said, passing a hand over his face. He was trying to make sense of what his brother was saying, but it was early and he felt as if his brain was still in a fog. It didn't help that his fingers still smelled from the woman. He dropped his hand away from his face and tried to put her out of his mind.

Last night before retiring to his room with the woman—her name was Janet, one of the girls who worked in the Coliseum—he had drunk too much, and now he was feeling the effects. It was his own fault. He never should have had a whiskey with Frank yesterday afternoon. Jim Manning and whiskey never got along that well. That was why he preferred to drink brandy. Once he'd had that one whiskey with Frank, he hadn't stopped. He was paying the price now.

"Did you keep drinking after I left yesterday?" Frank asked him. "You know you shouldn't—"

"Never mind," Jim said. "Just explain to me what the hell you're talkin' about."

"Jim—," Frank said, then stopped, thought and started again. "I sent for a man who will go up against Clint Adams for us."

"For money?"

"Of course, for money."

"Who is he?"

"His name is Duncan," Frank said.

"First name or last name?"

Frank shrugged. "All I've ever known is Duncan. What the hell does it matter if it's his first name or his last?"

"It doesn't," Jim said, waving his hand. He didn't want to argue with Frank today.

"Is he good, Frank?"

"With a gun?" Frank said. "Yeah, he's very good."

"Good enough to take care of the Gunsmith?"

"With the backup we're going to give him," Frank answered, "he should be more than good enough. All he needs is an edge—a small edge."

"Is he reliable?"

"Who's reliable, Jim?" Frank asked. "If we pay him enough, he'll do the job."

"Well," Jim said, his mind clearer now and getting into the swing of things, "we should certainly be able to take care of that, shouldn't we?"

Frank nodded and said, "At least that."

TWENTY

Clint continued to watch the stranger from his chair in front of his hotel. He followed the man's progress down the street and past the Coliseum. That didn't necessarily mean anything. The stranger kept walking, which meant he could have been going to Frank Manning's place, at the far end of town.

From across the street Clint saw Dallas Stoudenmire coming towards him. There was another chair next to his, turned to face the wall. He hooked it with his foot and turned it so Stoudenmire could sit.

"If I sit," the marshal said, "it ain't gonna look good for you."

Clint gave the man a long look.

"Sit."

Stoudenmire thought a moment, then shrugged and sat down. "Did you see him?" he asked.

"I saw him."

"Recognize him?"

"No."

"I checked my paper, but there's no poster on him," Stoudenmire told Clint.

"That doesn't mean anything," Clint said. "He could be very good at what he does."

"I know."

"This is the only hotel on this side of the border, isn't it?"

"Yes, it is," the lawman answered. "He went past the Coliseum, but he could have been going to Frank Manning's place."

"That's what I thought."

"I guess I'll just have to wait and see what happens," Stoudenmire said.

"I guess we will."

Stoudenmire turned his head and looked at Clint. "We?"

"That's what I said," Clint replied, looking straight ahead.

"You takin' sides, Clint?"

Clint continued to stare straight ahead. After a few seconds he sighed and looked over at Stoudenmire. "I never could mind my own damned business."

"Well," Stoudenmire said, rocking his chair back on its hind legs, "lucky for me, I guess."

"Wait and see."

TWENTY-ONE

When Duncan walked into Frank's Saloon Frank Manning was waiting at the bar. There were some other men in the saloon, all of whom worked for the Manning brothers. They would be Duncan's backup.

"Duncan," Manning said as the man approached.

"Frank."

Duncan was a tall, well-built man in his thirties. He was exceptionally good with a gun and hired out specifically to use it. He had never, however, done anything to get his picture on a Wanted poster. When he worked he was damned careful about that.

"A beer?" Frank asked.

"Sure."

The fat bartender drew a cold beer and put it on the bar for Duncan. Duncan drank half and put the mug down on the bar.

"Your message said this job was special," he said to Frank.

"It is," Frank said. "You have no idea how special it is."

After a moment Duncan said, "Well? I'm not good at guessing, Frank. Suppose you just go ahead and *tell* me how special it is?"

His tone betrayed some annoyance. Frank Manning had used Duncan many times before, and he always told himself that he was the employer, and Duncan, the employee. He always told himself that the man did not scare him.

He was always wrong, and this time was no exception. Duncan was a dangerous man to fool with. He was too cool for Frank's liking. Frank liked a man to have a temper, because a temper helped blow off steam. Hell, he was that way himself.

Duncan never blew off steam. He was always in control, and that made someone like Frank Manning nervous, because he couldn't understand a man like that.

Frank hesitated a moment, then leaned forward and said, "Clint Adams."

Duncan did not react. When he finally moved it was to pick up his beer and finish it.

"Didn't you hear me?" Frank asked. "The goddamned Gunsmith!"

"I heard you," Duncan said.

"Well?"

"It's gonna cost you."

"I know that."

"No," Duncan said, putting down the empty mug, "I mean it's gonna cost you—big!"

Frank frowned and asked, "How big?"

Duncan stared at him, his face expressionless. Then he said, "Get me another cold beer and we'll talk about it."

"Where is he?" Jim Manning asked Frank.

"Upstairs at my place," Frank said. "He's got a bottle of whiskey and a girl."

"What the hell good is he gonna do us drunk?" John asked.

"He's got to relax a little before he does anything," Frank responded. "Besides, he won't get drunk. I've seen the man drink and drink, and I've never seen him drunk yet. It's . . . amazing."

"When will he be ready to go?" asked Jim.

"Anytime after tomorrow."

"How about tomorrow?"

Frank flicked a look at John, who just shrugged. It was apparent that John didn't have much input into what was going on. It was obviously Jim's play. Well, that was fine with Frank, because if it didn't work this time, the next play would be his.

"I guess he could do it tomorrow," Frank said.

"What about the other men?" John asked.

"They'll be ready when I tell them to be ready," Jim replied.

"Okay, then," said Frank. "Tomorrow it is. I'll go and tell him now."

He started for the door, then stopped as he had

a second thought. "Uh, or maybe I'll wait until he's finished with the girl."

"I thought he was working for us?" John asked. "Don't tell me you're afraid of him?"

Frank looked at John. "You're damned right I am. If you're not, then you go and interrupt him while he's indulging in his pleasures."

John frowned and looked away.

"I didn't think so," Frank said, satisfied. He turned to Jim and added, "I'll talk to Duncan later and get back to you."

"Fine," Jim said. "Are the other men at your place, too?"

"Yes," Frank answered. "I'll talk to them, too."

Jim nodded. Frank glanced at John, then turned and left.

"You better find yourself something to do tomorrow," Jim told John. "Maybe something that will keep you out of town."

"Yeah," John said, "okay, sure. What about you? What are you gonna be doing?"

"Me?" Jim said, sitting back. "I'll be right here, doing business as usual. They'll be dozens of people around me when it happens."

"This better work," John said.

Jim frowned. He would have admonished his older brother at that moment, except that he was thinking the very same thing.

TWENTY-TWO

About midday Clint and Dallas Stoudenmire went over to the Top Dollar for a drink. They had used the morning to discuss different plans of action and had decided that the only thing to do was watch each other's back.

"I want you to know," Stoudenmire said over a beer, "that I appreciate what you're doin'."

"It's as much for me as it is for you," Clint said with a wave of his hand.

"No, I don't think so," Stoudenmire replied. "No matter what you say, you could still just ride out and save yourself a lot of grief."

"Dallas—"

"Just listen," the lawman said, holding up his hand to silence Clint. "I just want you to know that I appreciate you watching my back, and I realize that it can't go on for long—but I don't think it will have to."

"I agree," Clint said. "I think something will happen, maybe today, maybe tomorrow, certainly before the end of the week."

"Why do you say that?"

"Don't you agree?"

"Oh, yeah, I do," Stoudenmire answered, "but I want to know why *you* do."

Clint thought a moment, then said, "I guess it was something I saw in their eyes."

"Whose eyes?"

"The Mannings," replied Clint. "All three of them I met. The one called John, he looked scared. Frank, he had the look in his eyes of a man on the prod. But Jim, he's the one I'd watch out for."

"Why him?"

"Well, aside from the fact that I think he's the smartest—"

"You're right, there."

"—I saw a . . . burning in his eyes, a fever," Clint said. "I think if you put all of them togeth-er, you've got an explosion in the making."

"I agree, all right," said Stoudenmire. "In fact, I hope you're right. I'd like to put an end to this . . . this . . ."

"Feud?"

Stoudenmire frowned. "All right, for want of a better word, feud. I'd like it to end."

"Would they?" Clint asked.

"I don't know," the marshal replied. "Before I came along they were riding roughshod over everything. I'm the only competition they've ever had. If they kill me, they may end up being bored."

"Well, I think it will end soon, but I think you'd better expect a bloody ending."

Dallas Stoudenmire looked across the table at Clint. "That won't bother me none, Clint, believe me."

It was then, looking back across the table at the lawman, that Clint realized that Stoudenmire had the same feverish look in his eyes that Jim Manning had.

Shaking his head to himself, he wondered if he would *ever* learn to keep his nose out of other people's affairs. Here in El Paso he had gotten himself lodged firmly between two feuding factions—no matter what Marshal Stoudenmire said about the word "feud"—and he now felt that both sides were simply out of control.

Of course, he was on the side of "right" in siding with the law in El Paso, but he still did not know the beginnings of this confrontation. Stoudenmire was not "right" simply by virtue of being the law. Clint had known a lot of lawmen who had misused their authority in the past. He had not seen very much of Stoudenmire in action since his arrival in town, but just from the time he had spent talking to the man, the marshal seemed intent on doing his job the correct way.

Clint decided that he'd back Stoudenmire in the play that was about to come, but win, lose or draw, he'd be pulling out of El Paso when it was all over.

TWENTY-THREE

As the day wore on Clint and Stoudenmire began to think that nothing would happen that day. They started to think about how they would spend the night. They narrowed it down to two options. They could both sleep in Clint's hotel room, taking turns on watch, or they could sleep in the marshal's office, also taking turns on watch.

In the end they decided on the marshal's office. There were plenty of weapons there, and it was more defensible than the hotel.

They went to the general store—they had the owner open up for them because he had already closed for the day—and they stocked up on coffee and beef jerky and some extra blankets and ammo.

After that, they took up position in the lawman's office and split up the watches.

Over in Frank's Saloon Frank Manning had chased the customers out and closed early. Now the only ones in the place were he and his brother Jim, Duncan and the five men who would back Duncan's play.

"Anybody who wants out," Frank Manning said, "say so now."

"Tell them what they have to do," Duncan said. He was sitting at a table to Jim and Frank Manning's right.

Frank turned and looked at the hired gunman. "They know what they have to do."

Duncan stood up and faced Jim and Frank. "Spell it out for them."

He was looking at Frank, but it was Jim who spoke.

"Why don't *you* tell them, Duncan?"

"Okay, I will." Duncan turned to face the other five men. He said, "We're being paid to kill two men. Anybody have a problem with that?"

Nobody spoke until one of the men said, "That depends on how much we're being paid."

"Enough," Duncan answered.

"Okay," the man said. He looked around at the other men, all of whom nodded. "We're in."

"Okay," Duncan said, and before Jim could speak he added, "but let me make something clearer still. You five are being paid to kill the marshal."

"And you?" one of them asked.

"I'm being paid to kill Clint Adams," said Duncan.

There was silence all around. Then one of them asked, "The Gunsmith?"

"That's right," Duncan replied.

Somebody else said, "The honest-to-God real fuckin' Gunsmith?"

Duncan looked at each of the men in turn. "That's right. The Gunsmith."

A third voice called out, "How much are we bein' paid for this job?"

"Enough," Duncan said.

"Not enough to go up against the Gunsmith."

It didn't matter who said it.

"I'm bein' paid enough to go up against the Gunsmith," Duncan said, very slowly. "You five are bein' paid enough to kill the marshal. That's the way it is. Anybody object, say so now."

The five men exchanged glances, then looked at Duncan, who was staring very hard at them.

Nobody spoke.

Duncan turned and said to the Mannings, "Okay, now they know what they're up against."

TWENTY-FOUR

"This can't be an unusual situation for you," Dallas Stoudenmire said to Clint.

The marshal was seated behind his desk, Clint in a wooden chair in front of the desk. They each had their fourth or fifth cup of coffee in their hands. One of them was supposed to be asleep while the other was on watch, but they had lost track of who was supposed to be doing what. The fact of the matter was neither of them felt much like sleeping.

"That's true enough," Clint said. "Sometimes I feel like my whole life has been spent just waiting for somebody to shoot me full of holes."

"I dodged a lot of bullets during the war," Stoudenmire said, "and since." He hesitated, then added, "Some of them I didn't dodge fast enough."

"I've caught one or two myself, over the years," Clint said.

He stood up and carried his coffee to the window. He looked out onto the street, which was

dark and quiet. He was careful not to stand directly in front of the window, though. He would have
been backlit, and an easy target for whoever was
outside.

It was nearly three a.m., and the saloons would
be closing up soon. Clint turned and looked at
Stoudenmire. "What do you think will happen if
you can get rid of the Mannings?"

"Well," Stoudenmire said, "for one thing I might
be able to hire a couple of deputies."

"Even without the Mannings," Clint said, "this
town won't be a picnic."

"I know that," the lawman told him. "Still, most
of the people who live here are afraid of them.
With them gone, things would change, even if
only slightly—but definitely for the better."

"I suppose you're right," Clint said. He walked
back to his chair and sat down. "You should get
some sleep. I'm not tired. I can stay up and keep
my eyes and ears open."

"I just figured it out," Stoudenmire said. "I'm
on watch, and you should be asleep."

Clint looked down into his cup and said, "Well,
maybe one more cup of coffee."

TWENTY-FIVE

Over at Frank Manning's six men sat waiting. Duncan and Frank Manning sat alone at one table, four others at another. Jim Manning had returned to his own place. There was a knock at the door and Frank got up to admit the fifth man of the backup team.

"Well?" he asked.

The man looked at Duncan, not Frank. It did not escape Frank's notice that while he was paying the five men, it was Duncan they looked at as their leader.

"They're still inside the jail," the man said to Duncan.

"All right," Duncan said. "We'll take them when they come out in the morning."

"In the morning?" Frank protested. "Wait a minute."

"What's the matter?" asked Duncan.

"Well . . . this place won't be open, and neither will the Coliseum."

"So?"

"So . . . Jim and I need to set up alibis. If you hit them in the morning—"

"Wait a minute," Duncan told him. "You hired me to do a job, and I'm gonna do it. Don't start throwing obstacles in my way. It's up to you and your brothers to take care of your alibis. I can't worry about that. Shit, take women to bed with you."

Duncan stood up and walked to the door.

"Where are you goin'?" Frank asked.

"I'm gonna check out the area around the jail-house," Duncan said. He turned and looked at the five men seated at the other table. He pointed to the one who had just come back. "What's your name?"

"Stack," the man answered, "Andy Stack."

"You come with me, Stack," Duncan ordered. "The rest of you stay here—and stop drinking! We'll be moving at first light. When the sun comes up I'll kill anyone I find drunk."

Duncan went out with Stack following closely behind him. The other four men carefully pushed away their glasses. Then, just to make sure, they got up and changed tables.

Duncan and Stack walked down to the jail-house. They stood across the street in the shadow of a doorway. From there Duncan, his eyes adjusting to the dark, asked Stack questions. What were the buildings on either side of the jail? What was across the street? What was behind the jail? Stack did his best to answer all the questions as precisely as he could. Duncan scared the shit out of him, and he wanted very badly to accommodate the man and stay on his good side.

Duncan looked at the lit-up windows of the jail, but couldn't see anyone inside. The marshal was smart enough to stay away from the windows, at least while the lamps were lit. Backlit, he'd have made a perfect target. As for the Gunsmith, he had to be a smart one to have stayed alive this long.

Once the professional killer's eyes had adjusted to the darkness he moved out of the doorway to take a look around himself. He was careful, though, never to move too close to the jail.

"Stay here," he told Stack, who remained in the doorway.

"Where are—"

"I'll be back."

Before Stack could say another word Duncan moved away. Stack swore that the man just seemed to disappear into the night.

"Jesus—," he said under his breath.

How could a man just melt away like that? Try as he might, squinting mightily, he couldn't find Duncan again. He started to worry that maybe the man wasn't coming back. What was he supposed to do? Just stay here all night and wait, or go back to the saloon?

Suddenly, though, Duncan was right back at his side. He startled Andy Stack so badly that the man literally jumped, his heart pounding.

"Christ—"

"All right," Duncan said, "I've seen enough."

"How did you do that?" Stack asked.

Duncan looked at him. "Do what?"

Stack licked his lips. "Uh, n-never mind. We goin' back?"

"Yeah," Duncan said, "we're goin' back."

They moved out of the doorway and started making their way to the other end of town, back to where the others were waiting at Frank Manning's place.

"You got a plan already, Duncan?"

For a minute he thought the man hadn't heard him. Then Duncan spoke.

"I've got something in mind," the killer said. "Yeah, I got a plan."

"What is it?"

Without looking at Stack, Duncan said, "I plan to earn my money."

TWENTY-SIX

At first light Clint and Stoudenmire were both still awake.

"What do you say to some breakfast?" Clint asked.

"You buyin'?" Stoudenmire asked. "This town doesn't pay me much, you know."

During the night they had fallen into an easy, almost familiar camaraderie. The fever that Clint had seen in the marshal's eyes earlier in the day was not there during the night. He was sure, however, that if they had chosen to talk about the Mannings during the night—which they had not—that the feverish gleam would have been back.

"Sure," Clint said, "I'm buying."

"Let's go."

"Do you know someplace better than that cafe on San Antonio Street?"

"Sure I do," Stoudenmire said. "After all, I live here, don't I?"

They walked to the door together and Stoudenmire opened it. At that split second something slammed into the door near his head, and then they heard the shot.

"Down!" Stoudenmire shouted.

Both men had the same idea. Instead of ducking back into the office, where they would have then been trapped, they both went out the door, with Clint ducking to the left and Stoudenmire ducking to the right.

They each found some cover as a hailstorm of lead rained down on them, chewing up the door, the wall and the boardwalk around them.

And then, abruptly, it stopped.

"You hit?" Clint asked.

"No," the lawman answered, "you?"

"No."

"Somebody made a mistake," Stoudenmire said.

"I know," Clint agreed. "That shot was a little premature, wasn't it? Somebody got nervous and pulled the trigger too soon."

"Lucky for us."

Clint didn't reply. Somehow he didn't consider anything about their present situation to be lucky.

"There was too much lead flyin' to figure out how many shooters there were," Stoudenmire commented.

"I figure five," Clint said, "six at the most."

They looked at each other then, each sprawled behind some cover—Clint behind some crates, Stoudenmire crouched behind a horse trough.

"How do you figure?" the marshal asked.

"That's just the way it sounded to me."

"Okay," Stoudenmire conceded. "So where are they?"

"At least three above us," said Clint. "Rooftop or window."

"And?"

"The rest down below, across the street."

"You noticed all that?" Stoudenmire asked, in disbelief.

"Hey," Clint said, "maybe I'm wrong."

There was a pause. Then Stoudenmire replied. "No, I wouldn't bet on that."

"We've got to make a move," Clint said.

"We show our heads, they'll start firing again. They'll have reloaded by now."

"So we show our heads, they fire, and when they stop to reload again, we move."

"Okay," Stoudenmire agreed. "We go on three, all right?"

"Wait, wait," Clint said. "Is it *on* three, or after three?"

"What?"

"Is it 'one, two, go,' or 'one, two, three, go'?" Clint asked, wanting to get it straight.

"Jesus!" Stoudenmire exclaimed. "Now I know how you've managed to stay alive so long. It's 'one, two, three . . . go'!"

TWENTY-SEVEN

Duncan was livid.

One of the five idiots he was saddled with had fired too soon, and now Clint Adams and the marshal had found cover. It would have been easier if they had ducked back inside the jailhouse. At least that way they would have been pinned down. Neither of them was an amateur, however, and they had both known enough not to duck back inside the building.

When this was over Duncan intended to find out who fired that first shot—and that man was never going to fire a shot in error again. Right now, though, he had to make damned sure Clint Adams didn't come out of it alive. That's what he was being paid for. Let the other five worry about the lawman.

Duncan was at ground-level with two of his men. Two others were on the roof, while the last man was in a second-floor window. Duncan himself had not yet fired a shot, but now, as Clint

Adams and Dallas Stoudenmire stuck their heads up, he instructed the men on the ground to begin firing again. Once they did, the other three men followed suit, and once again the front of the jailhouse was being peppered with lead.

Duncan knew that this time, when the other five stopped to reload, one or both of the men across the street would make a break—and he'd be ready. If Adams made the break he'd make it with him. If the lawman made the break he'd send the other men after him, while he stayed here, on even terms with the Gunsmith.

He drew his gun for the first time, and waited.

Clint and Stoudenmire withstood the second barrage of bullets with little or no damage.

Stoudenmire felt something strike the back of his neck, but he knew that it was just slivers of wood blasted out of the building behind him. At worst he would end up with a few splinters and some blood on the back of his collar.

Clint suffered nothing more than ringing eardrums from the din, and when the shooting stopped it was even more painful to his ears, because it was so abrupt.

He said to himself, "Now!" and sprang from his cover just seconds behind Stoudenmire. As he did so he heard a shot and heard Stoudenmire cry out.

The lawman had been hit, but he didn't have time to concern himself with that. In a situation like this each man had to look after himself, especially since they had broken from cover and headed in opposite directions. He just had to hope that Stoudenmire was not hit too badly.

Duncan fired at the first man who appeared from cover without knowing who it was. As his shot struck the man he saw that it was the marshal and not Clint Adams.

"Damn!" he swore.

He saw Clint Adams then, a blur of movement as he scampered away from the jailhouse and found cover farther down the street.

"Hold your fire!" he shouted.

He turned his head and looked at the man nearest him, which was Andy Stack.

"All right, Stack," he said, "I winged the marshal for you. It's up to the five of you to finish him."

"Where are you goin'?"

"I'm goin' after Adams," Duncan said. "That's what I'm gettin' paid for." He pointed across the street. "I don't know how bad I hit the lawman, but I hit him. You should be able to finish him."

"How?"

Duncan looked annoyed. "Keep your men on the roof, call the man in the window down. You, him and the other man down here go across and *get* him!"

"Yeah, but—," Stack started.

"You're in charge, Stack," Duncan said, cutting the man off. "You mess this up and I'll come for you."

"I can't—" Stack started to protest, but Duncan wasn't there anymore. He had left his cover to move farther down the street.

Stack realized that if he didn't make this happen, if he and the others didn't kill Stoudenmire, then Duncan would kill *him*.

He couldn't afford to fail.

Stack turned to the man nearest him, Lee. "We got to get Harry down from the second floor."

At that moment there was a shot, the sound of broken glass, and then a man was falling from the window. He struck the ground right in front of Andy Stack. He lay there with his neck at an odd angle, his eyes wide open and lifeless.

"Harry's down," Lee said.

"Shit," Stack said aloud, and then thought, this ain't gonna be easy.

TWENTY-EIGHT

It was Clint who had managed to get off a shot at the man in the window. That's because his target had chosen that moment to lean out. Clint fired once and the man reared up and fell out, taking the window with him.

At the same time Clint saw another man moving laterally across the street until he was directly across from him. He couldn't be sure, but Clint thought it was the stranger who had ridden in yesterday.

He wondered now if the stranger had been brought in specifically for him. If that were the case, then Stoudenmire, now wounded, was going to have to face at least four men by himself—unless Clint could get near enough to him to help.

Clint made a move to go back the way he came but ducked back behind cover as two shots were fired from across the street.

"Can't go back the way you came, Adams," a voice shouted. "The marshal's just gonna have to fend for himself over there."

"Who are you?" Clint called out.

"Me? I'm the man who's gonna kill the famous Gunsmith."

"You got a name?"

There was a moment of silence, and then the man answered, "It's Duncan."

"Never heard of you," Clint called out.

"That's okay," Duncan said. "I'm gonna kill you, anyway."

"Well, come ahead, then," Clint told him. "Let's get it over with."

There were some shots from the other direction, and Clint knew that Stoudenmire wouldn't be able to last long without help—especially if he were wounded.

"We're in no hurry, Adams," Duncan called out. "Sounds like the lawman's in a little trouble, though."

Clint knew that. He also knew he couldn't afford to play games with Duncan. He had to do something unexpected to draw the man back; that meant going back the way he had come, back towards the jail.

Abruptly he sprang to his feet, turned and ran.

Across the street the move caught Duncan by surprise. He was sure he had Clint Adams convinced that he couldn't go back that way.

"Don't try it!" he shouted, but Clint was already moving.

"Shit," Duncan said, and stood up to get a clear shot.

• • •

Clint took three or four quick steps, and then turned very quickly to face the man across the street. Duncan had stood up to take his shot, and Clint knew he had take *his* first. He pulled the trigger on his double action Colt twice and Duncan staggered back as both bullets struck him in the chest. He kept back-pedalling until he struck the store window behind him, crashed through it and lay sprawled in the middle of a display of dresses.

Clint turned and ran towards Stoudenmire. Shots were being exchanged now and as he looked up he saw two men on the roof, standing and firing down at Stoudenmire with their rifles. He raised his gun, pointed it at one of the men and pulled the trigger. Clint's philosophy of firing a gun was simple. You *pointed* it as if it were an extension of your finger, you never *aimed*. His single shot struck the man in the head and dropped him.

He kept running, and as the second man on the roof swung around to take a bead on him with his rifle, he fired once and finished him, too.

That meant that all the trouble was now on the ground.

Duncan's bullet struck Stoudenmire in the side, and the marshal cried out and went down to one knee.

"Damn!" he swore.

He sprawled on the ground and immediately probed for the wound. He'd been shot enough to know that it wouldn't be serious if he could get it treated fast enough.

He rolled off the boardwalk into the street and stayed on his back with his hands crossed over his chest. Somebody was going to have to come and take a look, and he'd be ready for him.

He heard a couple of shots from down the street and then more shooting near the place where he had fallen.

He was lying on the ground, almost beneath a buckboard that someone had left unattended. The buckboard had one horse hitched to it, and the animal shifted nervously but didn't move. Stoudenmire turned his head and was able to see across the street beneath the buckboard.

The first thing he saw was a man fall to the ground, probably from the roof or a window. He silently thanked Clint Adams for that one.

As he waited he saw two men ease themselves into the street. One of them turned and made some hand signals, probably to the men on the roof. Immediately, they started firing.

The two men on the ground began to move across the street towards the front of the jail. They moved in a crouch, making steady progress, and Stoudenmire decided that he'd be better off *under* the buckboard. He crawled underneath, rolled over and waited there, lying on his belly.

Eventually, he heard the two men mount the boardwalk on his side, and he knew it was time to move . . .

• • •

Clint was approaching the front of the jail when he saw the backs of the two men. At the same time he noticed Stoudenmire come rolling out from beneath the buckboard. He rolled once, onto his back and to his stomach again, and then he was firing. The two men never had a chance. Stoudenmire fired until his gun was empty, and the two men danced backwards and then fell to the ground.

Clint moved quickly, checking them to make sure they were dead.

"Are you all right?" he asked Stoudenmire.

"I'm hit," the lawman said, "but check the others, make sure they're all dead."

"I'll be back."

Clint hurried across the street. The man who had fallen from the window was dead, either from his bullet or from the broken neck he'd suffered when he hit the ground. He rushed down the street to check Duncan, and found that he was dead, too. His body was riddled with cuts from the shattered window, but he was dead from the two bullets Clint had put in his chest.

Next he went into the building across the street from the jail and went up to the roof. Both men he had shot up there were dead, and there was no sign that there might have been others. He hurried back down to Dallas Stoudenmire's side.

"How bad?" Clint asked, crouching by the man. The marshal's entire side seemed to be covered with blood. He had his hand pressed tightly to the wound. His face was pinched and colorless.

"I've got the bleeding under control," he said. "If you can get me to the doctor soon enough, I may be able to dance again."

"Well, then, let's do it," Clint said, sliding his hands beneath the man's arms to help him up, "because that I got to see."

TWENTY-NINE

Clint half carried, half dragged Stoudenmire over to the doctor's office. The lawman kept complaining that he was all right, that he had been shot many times before and he could walk fine, but each time Clint started to let go of him, his legs just wouldn't hold him up.

In the doctor's office the elderly doctor told Clint to bring Stoudenmire into his examination room. Together they removed the man's shirt and trousers. The boots had to go, too, so that the pants could be removed.

As he began his examination the doctor asked Clint not to leave. "I may need you to hold him down," the doctor said, "or if he passes out, to move him around for me."

"I ain't gonna pass out," Stoudenmire said, his tone annoyed. "I've been shot plenty of times before."

Now that Stoudenmire was almost naked Clint could see that what he was saying was true. The man's body was a virtual map of scars from old wounds, made by both knife and bullet. Each time Clint tried to count he would lose track when he got into the twenties.

Clint heard the clatter when the doctor dropped the bullet into a basin. He then set about to control the bleeding, and when he had it staunched to his satisfaction, bandaged the wound tightly.

"All right," the doctor said, standing back and admiring his work, "just lie still there for a while. You want to tell me what happened?"

"You'll be able to find out all you want by just stepping out onto the street, Doctor," Stoudenmire answered. "Or by reading the newspapers tomorrow."

"In other words," the older man replied, "it's none of my business."

"Exactly," Stoudenmire said.

"Well," said the doctor, "maybe I'll just do that— step out onto the street, I mean." He turned to Clint. "Will you stay with him?"

"Sure."

"Must be some men outside who need looking at," the doctor said.

"Not by you, Doctor," Clint told him. "What they need is an undertaker."

The doctor frowned. "Well, I'll go and have a look, anyway. The undertaker is not above burying someone with a pulse if he can steal a fee that way." He looked at Stoudenmire. "Stay still for a spell. I'll be back to look at you in a little while. If it hurts, I can give you something for the pain."

"That's okay, Doc," Stoudenmire said, "I don't need nothin' for the pain."

"Suit yourself," the doctor said. "I'll be back in a while."

As the doctor left Stoudenmire looked at Clint. He must have been in some pain, but his face did not reveal it.

"What did you see?" Stoudenmire asked. "Recognize anybody?"

"No," Clint said. "They were all strangers to me. The leader was a man named Duncan. Apparently he was hired to take care of me, while the other five were supposed to kill you."

Stoudenmire made a face. For a moment Clint thought it might even be a grimace of pain, but it was not. The marshal was just annoyed—or perhaps it was just that his ego was hurt.

"That's not very flattering," he said in the next moment. His ego *had* been tweaked.

"Did you manage to get a look at any faces?" Clint asked.

"No," answered Stoudenmire. "I'll have to go over to the undertaker's later and take a look. If I can connect any of them to the Mannings—"

"I doubt that we'll be able to do that," Clint told him. "If the Mannings hired them, they probably stayed well out of sight and made sure they had real good alibis."

"Damn, I wish we'd been able to take one of them alive," Stoudenmire said.

"They didn't give us much choice in the matter."

"I know," the marshal admitted. "What bothers me is that we weren't ready for them. We waited all night for them to try something, and then we just walked right out into their gunsights."

"If somebody hadn't been a little too quick on the trigger, we'd probably be dead right now," Clint said. "We were careless, all right."

"We sure were," Stoudenmire agreed. "That makes me mad. Help me up."

"What?"

"Help me sit up!"

Clint went to him and helped him to sit up on the examination table. Stoudenmire's face whitened, but he didn't make a sound.

"You weren't kidding," Clint said.

"About what?"

"About having been shot before."

"Oh." Stoudenmire looked down at his scarred torso.

"It looks like you've led something of a charmed life," Clint commented, "including today."

"Charmed life?" The lawman frowned. "Somehow I never thought of it that way."

"Well," Clint said, "there's more than one way to look at everything."

"Except for this," Stoudenmire replied. "There's only one way to look at this ambush, Clint."

"The Mannings didn't strike me as cowards," Clint said, "but setting up this ambush—"

"Business."

"What?"

"They consider this good business," Stoudenmire explained. "Hand me my shirt."

"It's all bloody."

"I'll change later," he said. "Hand it to me."

Clint gave him the shirt.

"You're talking about the Mannings, of course," Clint said.

"Yes. They're behind this, of that there can be no doubt."

"What do you intend to do?"

"What *can* I do?" asked Stoudenmire. "I can't prove it, and if I just go after them I'll be flouting the very law I claim to be upholding."

"So you'll just wait?"

"For them to make another move," Stoudenmire said. "Hand me my pants."

Clint didn't bother telling him that they, too, were bloody. He just gave them to him. Clint didn't help him get into them because the lawman didn't ask for help. He simply watched while Stoudenmire pulled the trousers on over the bandage.

"But it will be their one last move, I guarantee it," the marshal said.

He'd successfully maneuvered his way into his pants and now set about adjusting them. That done, he looked up at Clint. "Next time I won't wait for proof before I move," he went on. "The time is gonna come, Clint, when all I do is take care of them."

Clint frowned and watched as Stoudenmire reached for his gunbelt and slung it over his shoulder.

"Come on," the lawman said. "I want to take a look at those dead men."

"The doctor said not to move."

"After bein' shot as many times as I have," Stoudenmire said, "don't you think I know what's better for my body than any doctor? I got to move around."

"Whatever you say. . . ." Clint followed him out the door.

THIRTY

The aftermath of the gunfight surprised Clint. Everyone in town seemed to be taking it so calmly, including Stoudenmire himself. Clint was glad that he had been there to help the marshal but wondered if the man wouldn't have found a way to survive even without his help. Above all, Dallas Stoudenmire had impressed Clint Adams as a survivor—even more so after seeing just how many times the man had been shot or stabbed in the past. While a man certainly could not be considered lucky to have suffered all those injuries, he could *only* be considered lucky to have survived them.

Before the day was out Clint made a decision. He'd stay a few more days, to give Stoudenmire a chance to stay off his feet as the doctor suggested, but at the end of the week he was going to leave El Paso. He had seen enough to know that it was not a town where he would like to spend much more time. It was too much like sitting on a powder

127

keg that had a lighted fuse.

Yes, it was time for him to leave El Paso and its feuds behind.

Jim Manning couldn't believe what had happened. In point of fact he had been in bed with a woman when the shooting started, without even realizing that he might need her for an alibi that morning.

When the first shots sounded the girl—another of those who worked for him at the Coliseum—sat up and looked around nervously.

"Did you hear that?" she asked.

"I heard," he said, not moving.

He was still lying on his back with his eyes closed, but his mind was racing. He wondered if Stoudenmire was even at that very moment lying in a pool of his own blood.

The girl—he couldn't remember her name, only that she had red hair and small breasts—looked down at him and asked, "Don't you want to see what it is?"

He wanted desperately to go and see what was happening, but he didn't want her to know that. He opened his eyes and looked at her wide eyes, the freckles on the bridge of her nose, the dark nipples of her delicate breasts, and reaching for her said, "No, I don't. Come here. . . ."

Frank Manning was also busy with a girl, one of those who worked for him, but since his place was at the other end of town he didn't hear the shooting. He just knew it was going on.

"What's the matter, Frank?" the girl asked. Her name was Ginger.

"Nothing, Gin."

"You seem distracted," Ginger said. She was a willowy brunette with incredibly long legs, pale skin and small firm breasts.

He took one of her breasts in his hand now and rubbed the nipple to life with his thumb.

"Not distracted," he said. "Not with you here, baby. Mmmm . . . ," he murmured as she slid her hand between them and wrapped it around his erection. Moments later she was busy at work there with her mouth.

He closed his eyes and tried to surrender himself to the sensations she was causing with her mouth and tongue, but a part of his brain kept wondering what was happening near the jail, whether or not Stoudenmire was dead.

Ah, what the hell, Frank thought as the girl continued to suck on him, his distraction was making him last longer, wasn't it?

John Manning didn't have a girl with him. He was sitting on his bed, fully dressed, listening to the shots that were coming from outside—he didn't dare go to the window to look.

He just sat on his bed and listened intently.

And then the shooting stopped.

THIRTY-ONE

Later, after the girl had left, Jim Manning paced the floor, waiting for word on what had happened. He didn't want to leave his room until he heard. Finally there was a knock at his door. He flung it open. His brother John was in the hall.

"It didn't work," John said miserably.

"What?" Jim demanded.

John Manning entered the room and closed the door behind him. He crossed the room and sat down on his brother's rumpled bed.

"I talked to Frank," he said, "and it's all over the street. They're all dead."

"Who is all dead?"

"Our men."

"And Duncan?"

"Yes," John said. "Adams killed Duncan, and then he and Stoudenmire killed the others."

"All of them?" Jim asked incredulously.

"Yes," John answered, "all of them."

"Jesus Christ!" Jim swore, running his hand through his hair. "And Stoudenmire? What about him?"

"He took a bullet," John replied, "but he's gonna be all right."

"And Adams?"

John shook his head. "Not a scratch."

Jim thought a moment, then exploded. "Goddamnit! You know what this means, don't you?" he raged at his brother.

"I know."

"We're gonna have to wait now," Jim went on.

"But Frank said—"

"We'll have to control Frank," Jim said. He was talking more to himself than to John. In fact, it was almost as if his brother wasn't in the same room with him. "We have to wait," he went on, "and plan before we can move against him again. Goddamnit, *this* was supposed to be the last time. *This* time it was supposed to work!" The last statement he made looking directly at his brother, once more aware of his presence.

John nodded mournfully. "I know."

Jim sat down on his bed. "Do you think he'll come after us?" he asked his brother.

"He can't prove anything, Jim," John said. "They're all dead."

Jim sat and thought for a few moments, then shook his head. "Six men." he said. "*Six*."

"I know . . ." John replied lamely. He couldn't think of anything else to say.

Jim looked up at John. "Next time we'll send an army of men—a whole goddamned army!"

Clint walked Stoudenmire down to the undertaker's office, where the bodies had been taken. Together they examined all five bodies, but Duncan was the only one they could positively identify.

"These others," Stoudenmire said, "they could be new, or they could have been in town all along. They're a type, they could be anybody. There's no way I can connect them with the Mannings."

"That figures," Clint said. "If they're concerned with good business, they'd make sure that was the case."

"Well, it might have been good business, but it was also a mistake. Could you do me a favor now, Clint?" Stoudenmire asked.

"Sure, Dallas."

"Get me to my office, okay?"

"You have to lie down."

"I'll lie down there," the lawman said.

"All right."

"And one more thing."

"What's that?"

"Stay away from the Mannings while I mend."

"I can do that," Clint agreed as he helped Stoudenmire out the door.

He could have taken the ambush personally. But he realized that it was truly meant for Stoudenmire, and that he, Clint, had just gotten in the way. Duncan, the man who'd been hired to kill him, had been taken care of. The Mannings he would leave to Stoudenmire. He would remain in town long enough for his friend to get stronger and then be on his way.

This was not his fight.

THIRTY-TWO

When he heard the knock at his door Clint could only think of two people it could be, and since he couldn't imagine Stoudenmire being up and around again so soon, that only left Wynona Jamison. But somehow he didn't think it would be her, either.

It was late, and he had personally bedded the wounded lawman down for the night. That was why he took his gun to the door with him. He stood to one side and held his gun ready. More than once he had seen how bullets could easily rip through a thin wooden door.

"Who is it?" he called.

"A friend."

Clint didn't know of any friends he had in El Paso except Dallas and Wynona, and this was the voice of a strange woman. He opened the door, still careful not to stand directly in front of it. When he looked into the hall he saw a very pretty blonde girl of about twenty-five smiling at him.

"I'm alone," she said.

"What do you want?" Clint asked.

"I want to come in, silly," she said, "and talk to you."

Clint opened the door wider and looked up and down the hall. Satisfied that she was alone as she had claimed, he opened the door wider.

"Come on in."

"Thank you."

He inhaled her scent as she went by him into the room. A combination of perfume and perspiration. She had obviously come right from work, and judging from the dress she was wearing, she worked in a saloon.

"I remember you," he said, for he suddenly did. He remembered seeing her, and he remembered where.

"You do?" She turned to face him.

"Sure," Clint said. "You work at the Coliseum."

"I'm impressed," the girl said. "I didn't think you noticed me."

"Oh, a man would have to be blind or dead not to notice you. You're the prettiest thing about that place, after all."

He walked to his gunbelt, which was hanging on the bedpost, and holstered the gun.

"That was a sweet thing to say," she smiled at him. "Thank you."

"What's your name?"

"Elaine," she said. "Elaine Mills."

"Nice to meet you, Elaine," Clint replied. "Did your boss send you here?"

"My boss?"

"Jim Manning?" he said. "Or *any* of the Mannings? They're your bosses, aren't they?"

She frowned. "Why would one of them send me here?"

"I don't know," he told her. "I'm just trying to figure out why you're here."

"Well, the reason is very simple," she said, eyeing him, "and it has nothing to do with any of the Manning brothers."

"It doesn't?" he asked. "Then it must be a pretty good reason."

"Oh, yes." She nodded sagely. "It's as old as the hills, too."

He had to smile at that. "Oh, is it?"

"Uh-huh," she said, nodding again. "It's a man-woman thing."

"Oh, I see."

"I was very interested in you when you came into the Coliseum," she explained, "and then even more interested when Sam Jones—that's the bartender?—recognized you."

Now Clint looked at her with real interest. "He recognized me, huh?" he asked. "This fella Sam Jones?"

"Oh, yeah," Elaine answered. "Of course, he wouldn't tell *me* anything about you, but he was in a big hurry to tell the bosses."

"The bosses?"

"The Mannings. Jim and John."

"Sam Jones, huh?" Clint commented, committing the man's name to memory.

"That's right," she said. "He was the bartender who was serving you that night."

"I remember him," Clint said. He made a further mental note to go and see Sam Jones before he left El Paso. "That still doesn't explain what you're doing here, though," he said.

"Well," she told him, reaching behind her, "maybe this will make it clearer."

She reached behind her back and unfastened her dress, which fell to the floor around her ankles. She was slender, with breasts that were round and hard like peaches. He felt himself reacting to her involuntarily—that part of his body often had a mind of its own. In fact, it had reacted halfway as soon as he had caught her scent when she moved past him into the room. It wasn't so much her perfume as her perspiration. It was a very natural smell, one he had always liked on a woman. He was not such a believer in the scents and colors women wore. He preferred a more natural look and smell of a woman. Now, with her standing fully naked before him, his body had reacted fully and completely.

She moved right up to him, and he thought he could feel the heat emanating from her body, right through his clothes. She put her hands on his waist.

"Do you still want to talk?" Elaine asked.

"We can talk," he said, putting his hands on her hips, "later."

He moved his hands up her sides, touching her only lightly, and then around to the front so he

could cup her breasts in his hands. She made a
sound in her throat and leaned her head back.
Her mouth opened in anticipation of his kiss and
he didn't make her wait. Her mouth was hot and
eager, and her hands were insistent as she undid
his belt. When she got his pants open she reached
in his fly and gripped him tightly.

"Oh, yes," she said, and then, "oh my, yes."

She went down on her knees then, yanking his
pants down so that his rigid penis was exposed.
She looked at it for a moment, her eyes bright,
and licked her lips. He felt her hand go around
him again, and then she bent her head and took
him inside her mouth.

He withstood the pleasure as long as he could,
then put his hands beneath her arms and lifted
her to her feet. He kissed her hard, mashing
his mouth against her and palming her perfect
breasts. She moaned into his mouth and ran her
hands over him. . . .

THIRTY-THREE

Elaine Mills was Clint's bedmate for the next three days—his last three days in El Paso. She came to his room after work, stayed with him all night, and left to go back to her room each morning.

"A girl needs her beauty sleep," she told him, "and if I stay around you I won't get *any* sleep."

That first night together she had told him that she had her eye on him from the first night he walked into the Coliseum. After that she would see him around town, but she knew that he was a concern to her bosses. That influenced her into staying away from him. However, when he was almost killed she decided that she was wasting an opportunity.

On the morning of the day he was to leave he awoke with her mouth working its magic between his legs.

"Jesus, Elaine—" he said, lifting his head off the pillow so he could look down at her.

"Shh," she said, "I'm having my breakfast . . ."

He let his head drop back to the pillow and said, "Oh God . . ."

After Elaine left he got up and got dressed. They had said goodbye.

"I'm not a clinging female, Clint," she had said, "and I'm really not all that sentimental. I just didn't want to miss the opportunity, that's all."

"Well, I think we both made the most of the opportunity, don't you?" Clint had answered.

She had given him a lascivious smile. "Definitely."

When he was dressed he took his gear downstairs and checked out. He hadn't seen any of the Mannings since the day of the shooting, but then he hadn't gone into any of their places, either.

When he left the hotel he went over to the marshal's office at the house. He knew Stoudenmire would be there. Three days away was certainly all that the lawman could take—and Clint had been surprised that the man had given in even that much.

When he entered the office Stoudenmire was seated behind his desk.

"Leaving?" the marshal asked.

"Soon," Clint said, dropping his saddlebags to the floor. "I've just got one thing to do. Mind if I leave my gear here?"

"No," Stoudenmire answered. "What do you have to do?"

"Pay a debt," Clint said. "I won't be long."

He left the office and headed towards the Coliseum. Elaine had told him that Sam Jones would be working early that morning. Each bartender had to take a turn cleaning up behind the bar, and they usually did that early in the mornings.

Clint walked up to the twin front doors of the Coliseum and pounded hard. Abruptly the doors swung inward and an annoyed Sam Jones appeared.

"What the hell—," Jones was sputtering. "We ain't open—"

Clint grabbed the younger man by the shirt front, and it was at that moment that Sam Jones recognized him.

"Hey, wait a minute—"

"I understand you recognized me the first time I came in." Clint put his face right up against Jones's.

"Well," Jones said, "I saw you once, when I was . . . younger." He was starting to sweat profusely.

"Couldn't wait to give the word to your bosses, could you?" Clint said.

"H-hey," Jones stammered, "a-after all, they're m-my bosses. N-no hard feelings, huh?"

"You're sweating, Sam."

"It's, uh, h-hot—"

"You need a bath."

Clint pulled the young man out of the doorway and practically dragged him into the street to a full horse trough.

"Whataya gonna do?" Jones demanded, his eyes

wide with fear. "You ain't g-gonna kill me, are y-you?"

"Not unless you can't swim."

"W-what?"

"Can you?"

"S-swim? Uh, n-no—"

"Well," Clint said, "I don't think you'll drown."

"What?—hey!"

Still holding on to his shirt, Clint grabbed Sam's crotch with his other hand and, lifting him off his feet, dropped him into the horse trough. He left him there, thrashing around trying to get to his feet and sputtering.

When he returned to the marshal's office Stoudenmire was out front. He had watched the whole thing.

"Was that your debt?"

"That was it," Clint said. He ducked inside to pick up his saddlebags and rifle, then came back out.

"I'd walk you to the livery," Stoudenmire said, "but I'm still pretty stiff."

"No problem."

Stoudenmire stuck his hand out and Clint took it. The two men shook hands warmly.

"Thanks for your help, Clint."

"My pleasure, Dallas," Clint told him. "I hope you get everything . . . resolved here."

"Don't worry," Stoudenmire said, "I intend to."

"Good luck."

Clint went to the livery, saddled Duke and rode out of El Paso. He hoped that in the near future he wouldn't read about Dallas Stoudenmire in the newspapers. He knew that was a futile hope, though. Once the fuse hit the powder keg here in El Paso, he knew he'd be reading about his new friend, one way or another.

INTERLUDE

Over the next few months, wherever he was Clint Adams read the newspapers religiously. He was still waiting for the top to blow of off El Paso. And so he became aware of what was happening during this span of time all over the West.

On April 28, in Lincoln, New Mexico, Billy the Kid shot his way out of jail. Pat Garrett, who had arrested Billy in the first place, took up the hunt for the Kid and on July 14 of that same year, in Fort Summer, New Mexico, a legend died as Pat Garrett shot and killed Billy the Kid.

There was some speculation as to the Kid's real name. Some said it was William Bonney, others claimed it to be Henry McCarty. One thing was known for sure, though. The day he died he was no more than twenty-two years of age.

Clint was in Texas when he read of the Kid's death, sitting in Rick Hartman's saloon in Labyrinth.

"Billy the Kid's dead," he said to Hartman.

"I know," his friend replied. "I read it. You still checking the papers for word on the situation in El Paso with Stoudenmire?"

"Yeah," Clint said, folding the paper and dropping it on a nearby chair.

"It's been three months, Clint. Don't you think something would have happened by now?"

"I don't know," he answered. "Maybe . . . maybe it's all blown over, but I doubt it."

Clint stared at the newspaper he had just laid down. He hadn't realized that he'd folded it so that the headline about the death of the Kid was showing.

"Did you know the Kid?" Hartman asked.

"No," Clint said, "never met him . . . but I met Pat Garrett a couple of times."

"What's he like?"

"A hardnose," Clint said. "You know, he and Billy were friendly, and he still did what he had to do because of the badge. He's a lot like Dallas Stoudenmire."

"Well," Hartman said, "what with Billy being arrested, then breaking out, and then getting killed, if El Paso explodes it'll make for quite a year—especially if Stoudenmire gets killed."

"Yeah," Clint said. "Let's hope we get out of this year without anybody else getting killed."

Hartman decided to change the subject. "You still going to Tombstone to see Wyatt and his brothers?"

"I intend to work my way over there," Clint

said. "I'll probably make it by October."

"Wish I could go," Hartman said. "Tombstone sounds like quite a place."

"Why not come?"

Hartman shook his head. "I've got too much to do here."

"That's bull," Clint said. "You're turning into a hermit, Rick. You hardly ever leave this place, let alone go out of town."

"How would you know?" Hartman retorted. "You're not here all the time."

"I'm just judging by when I am here."

Hartman stared across the table at Clint, then spread his hands and said, "Hey, I have every-thing I want right here. Someday you'll find some-place like that, too, and you'll settle down."

"Somehow," Clint said, without hesitation, "I doubt that."

With his concern about Dallas Stoudenmire's well-being and the news of Billy the Kid's death on his mind, Clint Adams gave no thought to what the rest of the year might hold in store for him when he went to Tombstone, Arizona, to see his friend Wyatt Earp and his brothers, and Doc Holliday.

He had no inkling that the most famous "inci-dent" of that year was yet to come, and that he would have a front-row seat.

PART TWO

~

**TOMBSTONE, ARIZONA
OCTOBER 19, 1881**

THIRTY-FOUR

When Clint rode into Tombstone, Arizona, he was still thinking more about Dallas Stoudenmire and El Paso than he was about the Earp brothers and Tombstone. At that point he did not know that the Earps were involved in an even more intense feud with the Clantons and the McLaurys than the one between Stoudenmire and the Mannings.

Later he'd appreciate the irony of riding into the middle of two feuds within months of each other.

For now, he was still concerned about Stoudenmire but looking forward to spending some time with the Earps—especially Wyatt, who was one of his oldest and best friends. In fact, Wyatt, along with Bat Masterson and Wild Bill Hickok, was one of the men who Clint considered his best friends. Hickok was dead, and Clint remained extremely loyal and protective of his other two friends.

Clint had never been to Tombstone before. It was a good-sized town, and he had to obtain directions to the livery stable. It was on Allen Street, he was told, between Third and Fourth streets. Clint thanked the man and shook his head. He had no idea that Tombstone would be so big. He knew that Wyatt and his brothers, Morgan and Virgil, had been in Tombstone for more than a year before they were able to secure jobs as law enforcement officials. But the brothers seemed to be very pleased with the way their fortunes were going now—or, at least, they were when Clint had last received a letter from Wyatt. That had been in Labyrinth, a few months back, just around the time Clint had returned from El Paso.

Riding to the stable, Clint got the general lay of Tombstone. There were four main streets that ran east to west—Safford, Freemont, Allen and Toughnut. The north-to-south streets were numbered. Later he'd learn that they ran from Second to Seventh. There were other streets, but they were muddy, filled with holes, and Mexicans, and wild animals of both the four-legged and two-legged variety. For all intents and purposes the "city" of Tombstone was four blocks by six blocks.

Clint found the stable and stopped Duke in front of it. The sign over the double doors said O.K. CORRAL.

"Looks like as good a place as any for you to get some rest, Duke boy," he said to the big black gelding.

He dismounted and left Duke in the care of

the liveryman, and then obtained directions to a hotel.

On Allen Street Clint walked by places called the Crystal Palace, Campbell and Hatch's Billiard Parlor, the Oriental Saloon and, finally, the Cosmopolitan Hotel.

He entered the hotel, put his saddlebags and rifle down and looked at the clerk, who was smiling.

"Can we help you, sir?" the man said. He was in his late twenties, with hair slicked down and parted just off center, as if he couldn't get it exactly right. He also smelled of some god-awful toilet water that he probably thought made him irresistible to women.

"I need a room" Clint told him.

"Yes, sir," the desk clerk said, turning the register so Clint could sign in. "We have the finest rooms in the city, sir."

"I just need a room with a bed," Clint said, signing his name. "I don't need the finest, or the best."

"Uh, of course, sir." The man frowned. "I'm sure you'll be very comfortable, Mr., uh—" He turned the register around so that he could read the name. "Mr. Clint . . . A-Adams? Clint Adams?" he repeated, looking up at Clint.

Clint supposed that in a city that boasted the likes of the Earps and Doc Holliday, as well as— at one time or another—Luke Short and Bat Masterson, it was too much to ask that he would go unnoticed.

"That's right," Clint replied. "That's my name."

"Well ... sir ..." the clerk said nervously. He reached behind him for a key and held it out to Clint, who noticed that the man's hand was shaking. "H-here's your key, sir. P-please enjoy your stay."

"Thank you," Clint said, accepting the key. "I'm looking forward to a nice, quiet, restful visit with some friends."

Later, he would recall the irony of that statement, too.

THIRTY-FIVE

The black eight ball rolled slowly towards the upper right-hand corner pocket, slowing as it approached. It seemed like it was going to stop just before dropping into the hole, but then it teetered and fell in.

"Damn it!" Virgil Earp cursed.

"You'll get the hang of it, Virg," Morgan Earp told his older brother. "I have."

"I'll never get the hang of this stupid game," Virgil said, staring maliciously at the green felt-covered billiard table.

"Wanna go again?" Morgan asked him.

Virgil gave his brother a heavy-lidded look. "Double or nothin'?"

"We didn't come here to play billiards," Wyatt Earp reminded his two brothers from a chair in a corner of the room.

Morgan looked at Wyatt, who was older than he by three years, but five years younger than Virgil. Even though it was Virgil who was the eldest and wore the badge of a deputy U.S. marshal, everyone knew that it was Wyatt who was the head of the Earp family.

"We're here," Morgan said, "and the table's here. Who do you want to back?"

Wyatt looked annoyed but said, "I got twenty dollars says Virgil whips your butt."

"Oh-ho!" Virgil crowed. "You're on! Any other takers in the room?"

Since there was only one other person in the room, that meant he was talking to Doc Holliday.

Doc was only a year older than Morgan, but he looked ten years older. Formerly a dentist, Doc had come out West when he learned that he'd contracted tuberculosis. The climate in the West was good for him, but he still looked sickly and was given to frequent fits of violent coughing.

Doc turned his intense dark eyes on Morgan, saying, "I'll go for twenty."

"On me?" Virgil asked happily.

Doc nodded his head. "On Virg."

"You're throwin' away your money," Morgan warned him.

"We'll see," Doc said.

"I'll talk while you fellas play," Wyatt said.

"Go ahead," Virgil said. "I'm listenin'." To Morgan he said, "I'll break."

"Sure," Morgan said magnanimously.

"Things are starting to turn ugly with the Clantons and McLaurys," Wyatt began.

"Those fellas were always ugly," Virgil said. He sank two solid balls on the break.

"Huh!" Morgan said, less magnanimous now. "Luck!"

"There's word going around that the Clantons are planning to kill one of us," Wyatt said.

"Which one?" Virgil asked.

"I don't know," Wyatt said. Actually, he did know. It was he the rumor concerned, but he didn't want to tell his brothers that. They'd probably start keeping him under house arrest.

Wyatt saw Doc look his way and frown. Doc knew that the rumors were about him, but he kept his mouth shut. Doc was Wyatt's friend, and in point of fact had followed Wyatt to Tombstone from Dodge City, so intense was their friendship. If Wyatt wanted to keep the information from his brothers, that was his business. The former dentist turned gambler and—some said—killer just settled back to listen.

"What do you want to do about it, Wyatt?" Morgan asked, frowning as Virgil sank two more balls.

"I know what I'd like to do," Wyatt answered, "but we can't, because we're the law."

"Then what can we do legally?" Virgil asked. He sighted on another ball and sank it, and Morgan groaned audibly.

"Nothing," Wyatt said. "Besides, they got Johnny Behan on their side."

Behan was the man who had defeated Wyatt for the job of sheriff. The Earps knew that Behan was good friends with the Clantons and would probably cover up for them.

"Goin' against him would be like the law goin' against the law," Virgil commented.

"Virg is right," Wyatt said. "We have to wait for them to slip up."

"Those boys are always up to somethin' no good," Doc Holliday added. "If we're patient they should step in it soon enough."

"Meanwhile," Virgil said, lining up his last ball, "we'll just have to watch each other's backs real close."

He stroked with the stick. The white cue ball struck his last ball, which shot across the table and jumped into the corner pocket.

"That's it," Virgil said. Morgan never had a chance to take his stick off his shoulder.

"Hmph," Morgan grunted, casting looks at both his brother Wyatt and Doc. "I sure could have used somebody to watch *my* back *here*."

THIRTY-SIX

Clint came down from his room and paused a moment in the lobby of the Cosmopolitan. He was hungry, but he was torn between having something to eat in the hotel dining room or going out to look for Wyatt.

He walked up to the desk. The desk clerk looked up, startled.

"Uh, is there something wrong with your room, sir?" the man asked.

"No," Clint said. "I just need directions to the marshal's office."

"Marshal Earp's office?"

"That's right."

"Are you looking for Marshal Earp?"

"Actually," Clint told him, "I'm looking for his brother, Wyatt."

"Well," the clerk said, "you have more of a chance of finding Wyatt Earp at the Oriental Saloon. He deals there sometimes."

"I see."

"You also might find him at the billiard parlor."

"Well," Clint said, "maybe if you give me directions to the marshal's office and I find Marshal *Virgil* Earp, he'll be able to tell me exactly where Wyatt Earp is, huh?"

"Oh, uh, well, certainly, sir," the clerk said.

Clint listened carefully to the directions. He did not want to end up wandering the streets of Tombstone aimlessly. To say the least, that would be embarassing.

By the time the clerk had finished with the directions, Clint's stomach was groaning audibly. He decided to have something to eat before he started his search for the Earps.

"All right," he said when the man stopped talking, "thanks. If anyone comes in looking for me, I'll be in the dining room."

"Uh, is someone going to come looking for you?" the clerk asked. He had visions of himself having to duck flying lead.

"The Earps are expecting me," Clint said. "They don't know I arrived today, but they might come in and ask. It was them I was referring to."

"Oh, I see," the clerk said, breathing a sigh of relief. "Well, if they come in looking for you, I'll certainly tell them where you are."

"Thank you."

"Uh . . . but I won't tell anyone else," the clerk added in a whisper. "Is that all right?"

"That's fine," Clint whispered back and went into the dining room.

• • •

When Wyatt headed for the door of the pool hall Virgil asked, "Where are you goin'?"

Wyatt turned and looked at his brother. "Just going to take a stroll," he said. "Maybe I'll check the hotels and see if Clint Adams got into town yet."

"Did he say he was definitely comin'?" Morgan asked.

"He's coming," Wyatt said. "I just don't know when."

"Maybe he'll get here in time to help with the Clantons," Morgan said.

"It's not his fight," Wyatt reminded them. "I'll see you boys back at the house."

By that he meant the house that Virgil shared with his wife, Allie. At one time, both Wyatt and Morgan had lived there with their wives as well. It was generally considered to be the Earp meeting place.

"Don't go walkin' around town alone," Virgil said.

"I'll go—," Morgan started, but Doc Holliday got to his feet and cut him off.

"I'll go with him," he said, crossing the room to the exit. "You stay here and try to get your money back."

Morgan turned to look at Virgil. "I might need a gun for that."

Virgil fixed his younger brother with a stern look and said, "Don't forget I'm the law, boy."

• • •

Out on the street Doc asked, "Why didn't you tell them that the word was out on you?"

"You saw them now," Wyatt said. "If they knew that Ike Clanton was talking specifically about *me*, they'd never let me out of their sight."

"And that's bad?"

"I don't need a nursemaid, Doc."

"Sure," Doc said but did not offer anything more.

As they walked away from the pool hall on Allen Street Doc asked, "Which hotel are you gonna check?"

"The Cosmopolitan," Wyatt said.

"Why?"

"He'd pass it on the way back from the livery," Wyatt answered, "and it would appeal to him."

"What about what Morgan said about using Adams if we have trouble with the Clantons?"

"Like I said," Wyatt replied, "it's not Clint's fight."

"I'll be there."

"It's not your fight, either, Doc."

"I'm your friend."

"I know."

"Clint Adams is your friend, too," Doc said. "If a fight starts and he's here, you know he'll be there, gun in hand."

"I know," Wyatt said. "But it won't be because I asked him."

THIRTY-SEVEN

When the desk clerk at the Cosmopolitan looked up from his desk the first thing he saw was Doc Holliday coming towards him. Doc Holliday scared him, in both his known capacities—dentist *and* killer. He could cause intense pain as one and death as the other. It was only when the clerk saw Wyatt Earp enter the hotel behind him that he breathed a sigh of relief.

Both men approached the desk. It was Wyatt Earp who spoke.

"Henry, I'm looking for a friend of mine."

"I know," Henry said, nodding his head sagely, "the Gunsmith."

"Clint Adams," Wyatt corrected him. "Don't let him hear you call him the Gunsmith. He doesn't like it much."

"Oh," Henry said. "I'm sorry."

"Is he here?"

The man nodded. "Checked in a little while ago."

163

"Did you give him a decent room?" Wyatt asked. "He's a good friend of mine, you know."

"Oh, yes, sir," Henry replied. "He has a fine room, overlooking the street."

"Where is he now?"

"In the dining room, eating."

Wyatt looked at Doc. "Leave it to Clint to take care of the inner man before he comes looking for me. Come on."

"I'll wait outside, Wyatt," Doc said. "You know, keep an eye out."

Wyatt opened his mouth to protest, then decided against it. He knew that Clint and Doc had met before, but he also knew that they had not taken to one another. It wasn't so much that they disliked each other, there was just . . . well, *no* feelings between them at all.

"All right, Doc," Wyatt said. "We should be out pretty soon. I'll want to show Clint the Oriental, and the rest of the town."

"Sure," said Doc. "I'll just grab a chair and sit myself down in front of the hotel. You take as long as you want."

Wyatt watched while Doc walked out the front door, then turned and walked to the dining room. In the doorway he stopped and looked around the room. Most of the tables were taken, but he had no trouble spotting his friend. As he walked to Clint's table, he knew that he had been spotted as well.

Clint saw Wyatt as soon as he entered the dining room but did not let on. It was a game they sometimes played, each trying to catch the other unawares. It had never worked yet. They were both too careful for that.

As Wyatt approached it was Clint who spoke first. "Pull up a chair," he said. "I'll have the waiter bring another cup."

Wyatt sat and indicated the coffee pot. "Hot and black?"

"Just the way I like it."

Clint looked up at Wyatt for the first time and the two friends smiled at each other.

"Been a long time," Wyatt said.

"Sure has."

"Nobody's fault, I guess."

"Just real life getting in the way," Clint said.

"We got some catching up to do," Wyatt said. "I hope you're going to be around long enough."

"Well," Clint said, "I did plan to visit for a while—especially if there's easy pickings around."

"I'm sure you can find a game or two."

"I understand the Oriental has a pretty poor choice of dealers."

Wyatt gave him a quick look. "Who have you been talking to?"

Clint grinned. "It's all over the street."

"You come over to the Oriental and try me out," Wyatt said, "and you'll find out."

Clint turned serious and asked, "How's it been going, Wyatt?"

"Couldn't be better," Wyatt said. "Virg finally got to be marshal, and even though I wasn't able to get elected sheriff, I did manage to get myself a part interest in the Oriental."

"Oh, I thought you were just dealing."

"No, I have, um, a small piece of the pie," Wyatt said, and Clint had the feeling that his friend had a lot more of the pie than he was letting on. He didn't push. That was Wyatt's business.

"How are the others?" he asked.

"Virg's happy with his job," Wyatt said, "and Morg's just happy."

"Doc Holliday here?"

"Sure," Wyatt said. "In fact, he's, uh, out front right now."

"Doing what?"

Wyatt shrugged. "Just sitting."

Clint regarded his friend across the table and knew instinctively that he wasn't being told everything.

"Wyatt," he asked, "what's going on?"

"Look," Wyatt said, "you just got to town. Let me show you around, and if there's something I think you should know about, I'll tell you. Deal?"

Clint hesitated, then shrugged and said, "Deal."

"Are you finished eating yet?"

Clint looked down at the steak bone in his plate. "Looks like it."

"Then come on," Wyatt said. "We'll start with the Oriental and work our way down."

Clint called the waiter over and paid his bill. When the two friends walked out into the lobby Henry, the clerk, glanced over at Clint, then looked away quickly.

"What's his problem?" asked Clint.

"That's Henry," Wyatt said. "He's intimidated by reputations. Doc scares the hell out of him, and I guess you do, too."

"Not you?"

"Me?" Wyatt asked in mock surprise. "I'm a sweetheart. Who would be afraid of me?"

"Silly me," Clint said. "What was I thinking?"

THIRTY-EIGHT

When Clint and Wyatt stepped outside Doc Holliday rose slowly from the straight-backed wooden chair he'd been sitting in. His face was pale, and Wyatt knew by looking at him that he had just suffered a coughing fit.

"Adams," Doc said, his voice sounding raw.

"Doc," Clint said, nodding.

"Street's clear," Doc told Wyatt, who nodded.

"Doc, I'm going to show Clint around Tombstone a bit," Wyatt said. "Why don't you go and get some rest?"

Doc studied Wyatt's face for a moment, then said, "Well, maybe I'll go and get a drink."

"And some rest," Wyatt insisted.

Doc shrugged. "I can rest while I'm having a drink," Doc said. "I'll be at the Alhambra . . . if you need me."

"Okay, Doc."

Doc looked at Clint. "See ya later, Adams."

"Doc."

They both watched while Doc walked away. He appeared frail, almost slight. He appearance certainly didn't fit the reputation he had as a cold-blooded killer.

"He's still watching your back, huh?" Clint asked.

"Couldn't ask for a better watchdog," Wyatt said, " 'cept maybe you, or Bat."

"Have you seen Bat lately?"

"Sure," Wyatt said. "In fact, he was dealing here for a while."

"What happened?"

"Ed called him back to Dodge City," Wyatt said. "They had some trouble, and after that Bat left Dodge but didn't come back here. I'm not sure where he is now. Luke was here for a while, too, but he finally left."

"Bat Masterson, Luke Short, Doc Holliday and Wyatt Earp in the same town together?" Clint said. "Sounds like exciting times."

"Actually," Wyatt said, "it was pretty damned boring."

"Well, maybe things will liven up some in the future."

"I hope not," Wyatt replied. "I like it quiet, Clint. Me, Morg and Virg, we got our wives here with us, you know. You've got to meet my wife, Mattie."

Mattie was Wyatt's second wife, whom Clint had not met before.

"Come on," Wyatt said, tugging on Clint's arm, "I want to show you the Oriental."

"Sure," Clint agreed.

He thought that Wyatt sounded like a proud father wanting to show off a child. He'd never heard his friend like that before. He also knew that beneath the pride and the supposed contentedness was something else. He had seen the look that passed between Wyatt and Doc when Doc announced the street to be clear. It had been more than just a passing remark when Clint had commented that Doc was still watching Wyatt's back.

Something was brewing in Tombstone, most likely trouble, but he knew he was going to have to wait for Wyatt to tell him in his own time.

Of course, there *was* another option. He could just saddle Duke up and ride out, avoiding any trouble. If he had done that in El Paso, he would have been better off—and yet he had stayed there to help Dallas Stoudenmire, a new friend.

Here in Tombstone he was dealing with Wyatt Earp, certainly *not* a new friend. If he had learned anything from his long friendships—the ones he had with Hickok and Bat Masterson and Wyatt Earp—it was how to read his friends and know when there was something going on.

No, riding out was certainly *not* a viable option in this case. Not when the friend he was dealing with was Wyatt Earp.

THIRTY-NINE

Clint was suitably impressed with the Oriental Saloon, although it did not quite match the elegance of the Coliseum in El Paso. It was more along the lines of the gambling house in San Francisco's Portsmouth Square, though on a smaller scale.

"This and the Alhambra are the finest places in town," Wyatt said proudly.

"I can believe it," Clint said.

The house was spacious, with plenty of gaming tables spread out, all with house dealers. In a corner was a table that was covered by a green cloth.

"That's mine," Wyatt said, pointing. "Nobody deals on it when I'm not."

"What do you deal?"

"Blackjack," Wyatt replied, "or faro. It depends on how I feel. Come on, I'll get you a beer."

"On the house?" Clint joked.

"Of course."

They went up to the bar, which was polished teakwood with no glass rings on the surface.

Wyatt ran his fingers over the smooth bartop. "We keep it this way all the time."

"Beautiful."

Wyatt wagged a finger at one of the two bartenders, a heavily mustached man with broad shoulders and a barrel chest.

"What can I get ya, boss?" the bartender asked.

"Two beers, Dave."

"Comin' up."

Dave drew two beers and brought them back, setting them down carefully on the polished bar.

"Dave, this is a friend of mine," Wyatt said, making the introductions. "Clint Adams."

"Glad to meet you," Dave said, extending a hand. He had a powerful grip, but he didn't overdo it.

"This is Dave Brubank, Clint."

"Brubank?" Clint asked, frowning as he released the man's hand. "Why does that name sound familiar?"

Wyatt was grinning. "I knew you'd remember."

It came to Clint then.

"Wait a minute," he said. "Battlin' Dave Brubank? You used to fight heavyweight, didn't you?"

"I did," Brubank said, "but that was a while ago. It's nice that you remembered, though."

"Remember!" Clint exclaimed. "I saw you fight for the title once—remember, Wyatt?"

"Sure, I remember," Wyatt said. "That was in New York about eight years ago. If you recall, Clint,

you had a previous appointment after the fight—
with a lady, I believe."

"You're right," Clint said, enjoying the memory.
"It was a lady."

"Well, I went and met Dave here, and we stayed
in touch over the years. When I came to Tombstone I sent for him."

" 'Scuse me," Brubank said. "Somebody else
needs a beer." Brubank went down the bar to
serve someone else.

"Pick up your beer," Wyatt said, picking up his
own. "Let's take a walk."

Clint took his beer from the bar and followed
his friend, who was leading him across the room.

They stopped first at a table where a lovely
dark-haired woman was dealing to a full house.
That is, she was dealing *blackjack*, and every seat
at her table was taken.

Wyatt waited until she finished dealing the
hand. Then he said, "Excuse me a minute, boys.
Dru?"

"Yes, boss?"

"I want you to meet a friend of mine," he said.
As she came around from behind the table some of
the players started to complain, but when Wyatt
looked at them they subsided.

"Drusilla Barnes," Wyatt said, "this is a good
friend of mine, Clint Adams."

Drusilla Barnes gave Clint a frank look of
approval, her dark eyes taking him in just once
from head to toe, and then settling on his face.

"My pleasure," she responded. "Do you play?"

"Poker," he said. "Blackjack is not my game. I find it . . . boring."

"Well," she said, tossing a curtain of glossy black hair back over her shoulder with a practiced flip of her hand, "if you stay in town long enough, maybe you'll give me a chance to change your mind."

"It's possible," Clint admitted.

"Okay," Wyatt told her, "get back to these animals before they tear the place apart. Just remember, this man is a friend of mine."

"I'll remember, boss," she promised. "Nice to meet you," she said to Clint and moved back around the table.

As they moved on Clint asked, "Uh, you didn't just fix me up, did you?"

"No," Wyatt answered, shaking his head. "That'll be up to you. Dru's no whore."

"She's not, uh, I mean—you and she aren't—?" Clint stammered.

Wyatt laughed and shook his head. "No, not me. I'm on my second wife, Clint, and I think I'd like to keep this one a little longer. If you're interested in Dru, be my guest."

"Does she have someone already?"

"Not that I know of," Wyatt said, "but who can say? All I can tell you is that I don't know of anyone who's involved with her."

Clint took one more look over his shoulder at Drusilla Barnes's back and decided that he definitely *was* interested.

FORTY

"Where are we going?" Clint asked.

"The office," Wyatt said. "I'll introduce you to my partner."

Once more Clint followed Wyatt across the crowded floor and watched as he greeted a few people along the way. He also saw the looks that some of the men were casting at his friend's back when they thought that they weren't being watched. It occurred to Clint that Wyatt had stepped on some toes since his arrival in Tombstone. Either that, or there were just some people who didn't like him because of his reputation.

When they reached the back of the room Wyatt opened a door and they went in.

Inside, the office was impressive. The furniture Clint saw was leather—in fact, the room *smelled* of leather. One entire wall was covered by a deep burgundy curtain. It was the wall behind the large oak desk, and at the desk sat a man who was now looking up at them with a frown. On the desk, just to his right, was a glass of what looked like brandy.

"Wyatt," the man said, but he was looking at Clint curiously.

"Dick," Wyatt said, "I want you to meet a friend of mine. This is Clint Adams."

"Ah," the man said. "I've heard of you, of course." He made no move to rise or to shake hands.

"Clint, this is my partner, Dick Shandy."

"Mr. Shandy."

Shandy waved his hand and said, "Dick. If you're a friend of Wyatt's—and I assume you'll be around for a while?"

"A while," Wyatt answered for Clint.

"Then you might as well call me Dick," the man said.

"All right," Clint agreed, "if you'll call me Clint."

The man nodded and said, "Done?" He looked at Wyatt and asked, "Is there something I can do for you, Wyatt? I've got books to go through."

"No, Dick," Wyatt said. "Clint just arrived in town and I'm showing him around."

"I see," Shandy said. He looked at Clint. "I hope you enjoy your stay."

"I'll try."

"Come on," Wyatt said, putting a hand on Clint's shoulder. "I'll show you some of the town." He turned to Shandy. "See you later, Dick."

The man replied with a nod and went back to his ledgers, which which were spread out across the desk. The look on his face seemed to indicate that he didn't care whether he ever saw Wyatt again or not.

Clint followed Wyatt out, wondering if he had seen what he thought he'd seen.

They left their half-finished beers on the bar and Clint followed Wyatt outside.

"Where are your brothers?" Clint asked.

"Morg and Virg are over at the pool hall," Wyatt said. "They've discovered that game, and they're getting pretty good at it. They keep taking money from each other. Well, mostly Virg takes it from Morgan. Did you ever play billiards, Clint?"

"Can't say that I have," Clint said.

"You'd probably be good at it," Wyatt said. "You need a good eye and a steady hand."

"How about you?" Clint asked. "Have you become pretty good?"

Wyatt shook his head. "I haven't tried the game. I'm not interested. Come on, I'll take you over to Campbell and Hatch's. That's where they are. They'll be pleased to see you."

Clint had met Morgan only once, but he'd had a drink or two and fired a couple of shots with Virgil in the past. He'd be glad to see Wyatt's older brother again and become acquainted with the younger one.

FORTY-ONE

When Clint and Wyatt entered the pool hall Morgan was bent over the table, lining up a shot. Virgil saw the two men enter and strode toward them. There was a wide smile on his face, and his hand was extended outward.

"Clint," he said, "by God, it's good to see you. When did you get here?"

"Just a little while ago, Virgil," Clint said. He clasped the proffered hand and pumped it enthusiastically. Virgil Earp looked much the way he remembered him, and it had been even longer since he'd seen Virgil than Wyatt.

"Is that Morgan?" Clint asked.

"That's him," Wyatt answered. "He's filled out, huh. He's thirty, now."

"Thirty," Clint said. "He was what—eighteen?—when I saw him last."

"About that," said Virgil. "Watch him, he's trying to sink this ball to win the game. If he does, he'll win back half the money he's lost to me."

"You're not letting him win, are you, Virg?" Wyatt asked.

"Well," Virgil said sheepishly, "you know how Lou gets when he loses money."

"Lou is Morgan's wife," Wyatt explained to Clint.

"Morgan's married?"

Wyatt nodded.

"And Allie gets mad at me, too," Virgil said. "I mean, Lou will complain to Allie, and then Allie will start in on me—"

"Sunk it!" Morgan cried, triumphantly. He looked around for Virgil, didn't see him near the table, then spotted the three men standing by the door.

"You lose, Virg," he cried out.

"Come over here, kid," Virgil said. "Say hi to an old friend."

Morgan, frowning and wondering if his brother was trying to get out of paying him, put his stick down on the table and walked over.

"Hello, Morgan," Clint said.

Morgan frowned, and then his face brightened as he recognized him. "Clint!" he said. "By God, man, it's good to see you." He grabbed Clint's hand and started pumping it. He was a strong young man.

"You've grown, Morgan," Clint said, and it sounded inane even to him.

"Some," Morgan agreed. "When did you get here?"

"That's the last time you'll have to answer that question," Wyatt said to Clint. To Morgan, Wyatt said, "A few hours ago. He stopped to eat before coming to look for us."

"How long you gonna be stayin'?" Morgan asked.

"A few days," Clint replied, "maybe longer."

"Well, good," Morgan said, finally releasing Clint's hand. The younger man pointed at the pool table. "Maybe I can get you to play some pool while you're here."

"Poker's more my game, Morg," Clint told him. "I've never played pool."

"Uh-oh," Virgil said. "Don't worry, Clint, Morgan'll teach you, right Morg?"

"Right!" Morgan said enthusiastically.

"Uh-huh," Clint nodded knowingly, "and relieve me of some of my money while he's at it, huh?"

"Well," Virgil said, "he's got to make back from somebody what he loses to me, right?"

"Hey," Morgan reminded his brother, "I just won back half what I lost, remember? Come on, hand it over."

"Okay, okay," Virgil said, laughing. He dug into his pocket and handed his brother some money.

"Want to play again?" asked Morgan.

"Remember this?" Virgil pointed to the badge pinned on his chest. "I got to pretend I work for a living."

"Okay," Morgan said, "then I'll teach Clint—"

"Morgan!" Wyatt said, and his tone was sharp. "Go with Virgil."

Morgan stared at Wyatt for a moment, then said, "Oh, yeah, that's right. Okay, let me get my gunbelt."

He went back to the table and retrieved his gunbelt from a nearby chair. As he started past Wyatt to follow Virgil out Wyatt grabbed his arm.

"Don't take your gunbelt off again, Morg," Wyatt ordered. "Not until you get home. Understand?"

"Sure, Wyatt, sure," Morgan said. "I understand."

"See you later, Clint," Virgil called from the stairs.

Morgan tossed them a wave as he followed his older brother down the stairs.

Clint walked across the room to the pool table, ran the palm of his hand over the green felt. He walked around to where the white cue ball was and picked it up.

"What's going on, Wyatt?" he asked.

"What do you mean?"

Clint rolled the ball across the table. It struck the opposite end and rolled all the way back to him.

"I was going to let you tell me in your own time, but it's obvious that something's going on. Doc was watching your back, and now you just about bit Morgan's head off, forcing him to go along with Virgil. I assume they'll be watching *each other's* backs."

Wyatt frowned. "We always watch each other's backs, Clint."

But Clint knew the man was about to give in and tell him what was going on, so he remained silent and waited, rolling the ball back and forth across the table time and again.

FORTY-TWO

Wyatt told Clint a story about brothers named Clanton and brothers named McLaury, thieves all, whom the Earps were intent on putting out of business.

"They have the local sheriff, Johnny Behan, on their side as well," Wyatt added.

"The sheriff's crooked?"

"Well, not outright, but he's friends with the Clantons and the McLaurys and he hates us. He beat me out for the job, you know."

"Fair and square?"

Wyatt's face was expressionless when he said, "So they tell me."

"What's all this business about watching each other's backs?" Clint asked.

"Oh, that," Wyatt answered. "Ike Clanton's been passing the word that he's going to kill one of us."

"Which one?" Clint asked. "Virgil, because he's a marshal?"

"I haven't told the boys this because I don't want them nursemaiding me, and I don't want Mattie to find out."

"It's you?"

Wyatt nodded.

"So you've got Morgan and Virgil watching each other's backs, while Doc watches yours?"

"Right."

"Seems a waste of your brothers' time, Wyatt," Clint observed.

"Not necessarily," Wyatt said. "There's no telling what the Clanton gang would do to Morgan or Virgil, just to get to me."

Clint frowned. "This sounds like more than just the law against the lawless," he said.

"Well," Wyatt admitted, "there *are* some folks in town who are calling it a feud, but—what's the matter?"

Clint hadn't realized that his face gave him away when he heard the word "feud." It made him think of El Paso all over again, and that he was walking into another El Paso situation.

"Nothing," Clint said. "I just . . . don't like feuds much."

"Neither do I," said Wyatt. "I don't look at this as a feud, but like I said, some folks do."

"Anybody else involved besides the Clantons and McLaurys?" Clint asked. He had not heard of either set of brothers.

Wyatt nodded. "Johnny Ringo."

"Ringo?" *That* was a name Clint *had* heard. "Ringo's supposed to be a bad one, Wyatt."

"He is, believe me."

Clint thought for a moment. Maybe, he considered, Ringo's presence served to offset that of Doc Holliday. After all, aside from those two it seemed to be brothers on both sides.

"How many Clantons and McLaurys are there?" Clint asked.

"Ike, Finn and Billy Clanton, and their old man," Wyatt said, "and Frank and Tom McLaury."

Clint counted mentally. If everybody had a gun that made seven on the side of the Clanton gang, against the three Earps and Doc Holliday. "Odds seem a little off," Clint said.

"Well," Wyatt replied with a tight grin, "we ain't going to wait for them to get some more help."

"You know what I mean."

"It'll work out, Clint," Wyatt said. "Don't worry about it."

"Sounds like you could use another gun."

Wyatt shook his head. "It's not your fight, Clint. In fact, maybe nothing will happen while you're here."

"Maybe," Clint said, "nothing will happen at all."

"Well, I think that's a little *too* much to ask for," Wyatt said.

FORTY-THREE

Outside of town Ike Clanton sat on the porch of the shack that served as the Clantons' home. It was also the base of operations for the Clanton-McLaury gang—which most folks simply referred to as the Clanton gang. And while Old Man Clanton was the father of the three boys, it was Ike who was the acknowledged leader of the gang—just as Wyatt Earp was the leader of the Earp-Holliday faction.

Ike was sitting on the porch with Frank McLaury when they both saw young Billy Clanton riding hell-bent for leather towards the shack.

"Looks like Billy's got something on his mind," Frank said.

"Probably a gal," Ike said. "That's what my little brother usually has on his mind."

As Billy got closer Ike stood up. He could tell from the look on his younger brother's face that he had more on his mind this time than a new girl.

Billy reined in his horse and dropped down before the animal had completely stopped.

"What's got you so riled up?" Ike asked.

"I just come from town," Billy said, all out of breath. "The Earps' got company."

"So?" Ike said.

"Clint Adams."

Ike didn't say anything.

"The Gunsmith, Ike," Billy said, almost desperately.

"I know the name, Billy."

"Well, now they got the Gunsmith *and* Doc Holliday on their side," Billy said, "what're we gonna do?"

Ike put his hand on his little brother's shoulder. Billy Clanton was at that stage in life where he couldn't be called a boy, but he wasn't quite a man yet. He had a man's body, and a man's desires, but he still had a young boy's temperament.

"Relax, Billy," Ike told him. "All we know for sure—if your source is good—is that Adams is in town. We don't know why or for how long."

"Why is because they sent for him to use against us," Billy said impulsively.

"We don't know that yet, Billy," Ike said, "and there ain't no use in goin' off half-cocked about it until we do know for sure."

"But Ike—"

"Go take care of your horse," Ike said.

"Ike—"

"Go on, boy, do what I tell you!"

Billy's shoulders slumped, but he obeyed his brother and walked his horse away.

Ike turned and looked at Frank. "What do you think, Frank?"

Frank frowned. "I don't like it, Ike, but you're right. Until we know what Adams's part is, we can't get all excited about it."

"Where's Ringo?"

"Out with Tom, I think," Frank said. "Why?"

"You know Ringo," said Ike. "What's he gonna want to do when he hears that Clint Adams is in town?"

"Oh, yeah." Frank nodded. "He's gonna want to try him."

"We've got to find him and talk to him," Ike said.

"You talk to him," replied Frank. "You're the only one he listens to."

"All right," Ike agreed. "But you gotta help me find him."

Frank sighed but got up from his chair.

"All right," he said. "I'll saddle the horses."

"I'll be right along," Ike told him. "I got to talk to Pa."

Frank McLaury stepped down off the porch and walked away. Ike Clanton looked off into the distance and squinted, as if he were trying to see into the future. After a few moments he shrugged, gave up and walked into the shack.

FORTY-FOUR

Clint remained with Wyatt Earp for a while. Somewhat later they both walked over to the Alhambra to find Doc Holliday. They found the man sitting at a table alone, with a bottle of whiskey and a deck of cards.

"No takers, Doc?" Wyatt asked.

"It's early," Doc said. He looked up at Clint with interest. "What about you? Interested in a poker game later?"

"Sure," Clint said. "After dinner?"

Doc looked up at Wyatt, then back at Clint. "We'll have to play at the Oriental, though."

"I understand," Clint said.

Doc glanced at Wyatt for confirmation, and Wyatt nodded.

"I'll line up at least three more players, then," Doc said. He looked at Wyatt and asked, "How about you?"

"I'll be dealing tonight."

"Fine," Doc said. "You fellas want to have a drink before I leave?"

"Sure," Wyatt said, and Clint nodded and sat.

Doc waved his hand and one of the Alhambra saloon girls came over. She was about thirty, blonde, short and full-bodied with a bosom that was, one might say, prodigious.

"Mae," Doc told her, "bring my friends whatever they want and put it on my tab."

"Sure, Doc," she said.

She turned to look expectantly at Wyatt and Clint. Clint looked into her eyes and saw that she was perfect for this job. He had the feeling there was very little going on behind those eyes beyond what she was doing at that very moment.

"Beer," Clint said.

"The same," Wyatt added.

"Comin' up," she said and flounced away.

"She doesn't have a lot of brains," Doc said, watching her flounce, "but she makes up for it in other areas."

"Speaking of talents in other areas," Wyatt said, "how's Kate?"

Kate Elder, sometimes called Big-Nosed Kate, was the closest thing Doc had to a steady woman. She was a prostitute, but she seemed to work only when she wanted to. Most of the time she was trailing along after Doc.

"Kate's fine," Doc answered and his eyes told Wyatt not to press the joke.

Wyatt decided to follow the advice Doc's eyes were giving him. Doc sometimes had a habit of losing his temper without warning, especially when he was drunk, and although he'd never done so with Wyatt—or any of the Earps, for that matter—Wyatt was still careful not to push it. Also, Wyatt could see that his friend was more than a little drunk, although he doubted that Clint could see it. Doc held his liquor real well. In Dodge, Wyatt had seen Doc kill three men while he was drunk and they were stone cold sober.

Mae returned with their beers and asked if they wanted anything else.

"Not just now, honey," Doc said, patting her on the rear. "Thanks."

"Sure, Doc."

"So Wyatt told you about his, uh, situation?" Doc asked Clint.

"He did," Clint replied. "I told him it sounded like you were a little outnumbered."

"We are," Doc said. "You dealin' yourself in?"

"I told Clint that this wasn't his fight," Wyatt interrupted.

"He knows that," Doc said. "That ain't never stopped him before."

"What do you mean?" Wyatt asked.

Doc looked at Clint but spoke to Wyatt. "I heard some talk about El Paso a few months ago," he answered. "The marshal down there, Dallas Stoudenmire, had a problem much the same as yours. Adams here was there to help him out."

"Is that right, Clint?"

"I was there," Clint said. "I'd never been to El Paso, and I'd read some about it. Thought I'd go down and take a look. Stoudenmire was the

marshal. I met him, we got a little friendly, and
he had some trouble. I was there and I helped
him. That's all there is to it. I didn't *go* there to
help him."

"See?" Doc said. "So he's here, and he'll help
you out."

"If something happens while I'm here," Clint
said, "I'll help out, sure." He hesitated a moment
and then added, looking at Doc Holliday, "Is that
what you wanted to hear, Doc?"

"That's what I wanted to hear," said Doc. "Wyatt
here is too much of a gentleman to *ask* a friend
to take up a gun in his behalf, but he'll take one
when it's offered."

"So you thought you'd just force my hand and
make me offer, huh?"

Doc shrugged. He suddenly seemed to lose
interest in the conversation. He poured himself
another shot of whiskey, his hand shaking slightly. He downed it, then stood up and straightened
his coat.

"I better get going if I'm gonna set up that
game," Doc said. He peered owlishly at Clint.
"You're still interested in the game, aren't you?"

"Oh, yeah," Clint replied, "more than ever, Doc.
More than ever."

"Good," Doc said. "See you both later."

Wyatt gave Doc a dirty look which the other
man ignored as he walked away.

"I'm sorry, Clint," Wyatt told his friend.

"It's okay, Wyatt," Clint said. "He's just a little
drunk."

"I didn't think you noticed."

"Oh, I noticed."

"He usually holds his liquor pretty well," Wyatt said. "I guess we're lucky he wasn't *mean* drunk, yet."

"He should be by the time we play poker tonight," Clint said.

"No," said Wyatt. "Chances are he'll sober up by then. He likes to be able to see the cards when he plays."

"Wyatt," Clint asked, "you knew I'd help if trouble came up while I was here, didn't you?"

"Sure I did, Clint," Wyatt said. "I didn't ask because I knew I wouldn't have to. I just hope you leave town before it starts."

"You're pretty sure there will be trouble, right?"

"Not pretty sure, Clint," Wyatt answered. "*Dead* sure—with the emphasis on 'dead.' "

"Any idea how close you might be?"

"Well, if I wasn't so selfish I'd probably tell you to leave town now, but since you just got here I won't tell you that."

It suddenly came back to Clint how he had likened El Paso to a keg of dynamite with a lit fuse. Well, the same might have applied to Tombstone as well.

He just wondered how he always managed to get to these places just as the fuse was burning down.

FORTY-FIVE

Doc Holliday had no trouble finding poker players for the game that night. In fact, instead of three others, he found four, and the way he did it was to tell them that Clint Adams would be playing. Over the past few years Clint had developed almost as much of a reputation as a poker player as he had as a gunslinger. Of course, that reputation existed mainly among other poker players. To most people he was still known as the Gunsmith, a man who could almost do magic with a gun. That might have been another reason the other players agreed to play—that and the hard stare Doc Holliday had given them when he said, "We're playing poker tonight. Be there!"

Clint and Wyatt split up when Wyatt joined up with Morgan and Virgil. Clint went back to the hotel for a bath and a change of clothes. He decided to have dinner in the hotel dining room. He invited Wyatt and his brothers to join him, but they said they had to go to Virgil's house to eat and to talk. They invited Clint to come along, but he declined. He was not yet ready to meet the Earp wives.

After dinner he went to the Oriental Saloon. Doc and the other players hadn't arrived yet, and neither had Wyatt. He stopped at the bar for a beer. His eyes fell on Drusilla Barnes, who was working her table. Although it was early all but one of her chairs were taken.

"She's somethin', ain't she?"

He turned and saw Dave Brubank leaning his meaty forearms and elbows on the bar. The bartender was looking across the floor at Drusilla.

"She is that," Clint agreed.

"You know," Brubank said, "men come and go in here, and I lose count of the number of them who make a try for her. She just don't seem interested."

"Maybe she's just particular."

"Could be," he said with a shrug. "I know one thing for sure."

"What's that?"

"She don't like bartenders."

Clint laughed and walked over to the table with his beer.

"Mr. Adams," she said as if it were an announcement. "Just in time to fill an empty chair."

He sat down and looked across the table at her. Her hair was long, hanging past her shoulders. While the girls working the floor were wearing low-cut gowns, Drusilla was wearing a shirt, tie and vest. She still managed to outshine the others.

"The game is blackjack," she said, "minimum bet twenty dollars."

"Maximum?"

"Oh, there isn't really a maximum. That is, unless you're talking *big* money."

She was able to deal and hold a conversation without losing track of either.

"What happens then?" Clint asked.

"Then," she said, gathering in the bets because no one had beaten her that hand, "we have to get the bet okayed by one of the bosses."

"Wyatt Earp . . ."

She nodded, " . . . or Mr. Shandy."

There were four other players at the table and from the looks of them they weren't having much luck beating Drusilla Barnes.

"Well, all right," Clint said, digging into his pocket. "Do I need chips?"

"Money plays," she said and dealt him a hand along with the others.

He put twenty dollars down and looked at his cards. He had a king in the hole and a deuce showing. Drusilla—or the House—was showing a picture card.

Clint knew there were a lot of rules in blackjack—rules of thumb, mostly. Like when to split a pair, when to double down, and what to do when the dealer had a face card showing. He didn't play the game often enough, though, to know all those rules, so he decided he would just play the way he did most things—by instinct.

There was one player to his right, and three to his left. The player on his right took a card and busted. He folded his hand in disgust.

"Card, please," Clint said.

Drusilla dropped an eight on his deuce. That gave him twenty, enough to win most of the time.

"I'll stay."

"Hit me," the man next to him said, and she did—hard. He folded.

The other two players each bought a card and stood. Drusilla turned her hole card over. It was a nine of hearts.

"Nineteen," he said. "Pay twenty."

Clint turned his hole card over while everyone else folded.

"Well," she said, looking at him appraisingly, "beginner's luck."

She paid him, giving him back his twenty plus another twenty. That was one reason Clint didn't like blackjack; the payoff on a straight win was only two-to-one. If a player made blackjack—that is, 21—on the deal, he was paid two-and-a-half to one. That meant for twenty dollars he'd get back thirty. At that rate, unless he were betting large amounts of money, it was simply a matter of grinding out a profit.

He much preferred poker.

"What brings you back tonight?" Drusilla asked, gathering up the cards.

"A poker game."

"House game?"

"No," he said, "private."

She dealt out another hand. This time he got an eight in the hole and a seven on the table. He took a hit and busted when she gave him another eight for a total of twenty-three.

"You should have stayed," the man to his left said. Meanwhile, he took a hit on thirteen and busted with a picture card.

"Thanks for the advice," Clint said.

"You playin' poker with Doc?" Drusilla asked Clint.

When he looked at her he saw that she was looking past him. He turned and saw that Doc Holliday had just entered the place. Idly he wondered why no one was worried about watching Doc's back. He was, after all, known to be good friends with Wyatt Earp.

"I guess it's time for you to play, huh?" Drusilla asked.

"You playin' poker with Doc Holliday?" the man to his left asked. He was the man who was giving him advice on blackjack.

"That's right."

"Better make sure he's sober before you sit down," the man advised. "Doc's pretty mean when he's drunk—especially when he's losin'."

"Is that a fact?"

"It surely is," the man said. Then a thought struck him. "Uh, have you, uh, played poker with Doc before?"

"Oh, sure," Clint replied, sliding off his seat. "Doc and I are old friends."

"Oh, uh—" the man stammered, "I, uh, didn't mean no offense—I mean, you won't tell Doc what I said, uh, will ya?"

"No," Clint said, and then smiled at the man and said, "not unless he asks." He gave Drusilla a more genuine smile. "We're even," he said.

"After two hands," she reminded him. "Come back for more."

It sounded like an invitation.

"I will," he said. "You can count on it."

She gave him a smile that would have melted ice. He reluctantly turned away and walked over to where Doc was standing.

FORTY-SIX

"Ready to play, Doc?" Clint asked.

Doc looked at him with eyes that Clint could only describe as "dead." He knew all about Doc's disease, and he knew that even Doc considered himself to be nothing more than a walking dead man, just marking time. Still it was disconcerting to look into the man's eyes that way and actually *see* it.

"When the others get here," Doc answered. "We can sit at the table, though, and have a drink. I want to talk to you first."

"Okay," Clint said. "I have a beer."

Doc turned to the bar and told Dave Brubank, "A whiskey."

Clint was glad the man hadn't asked for the whole bottle.

When Doc had his whiskey he led the way to a table. It was situated in a corner in such a way that both men were able to sit with their backs to a wall. Also, they both had a clear view of the table Wyatt Earp would be dealing at that night.

"About this afternoon," Doc began.

"What about it?"

Doc hesitated. When he finally spoke he seemed to be forcing the words out. "I may have been out of line."

"I don't think so."

"What?"

"I don't think you were out of line, Doc," Clint said. "Sure, you put my back against the wall, but I know why you did it."

Doc frowned. "Why?" he asked.

"Because you're Wyatt's friend, Doc," Clint replied. "I know that. Maybe you're even his best friend."

Doc apparently didn't know what to say to that, so he maintained a rather confused silence.

"Look, you knew he'd have a better chance of survival with me *and* you backing his play. I have to tell you, though, you didn't force me into anything. I'm his friend, too, Doc. If there's trouble, I don't need you to tell me to be there for him."

Doc stared at Clint for a couple seconds, then abruptly looked past him. "The others are here," he said. His eyes met Clint's again. "Look, I . . ."

"Forget it, Doc," Clint told him. "Let's just play cards."

FORTY-SEVEN

Clint played poker with Doc and the others for five hours. During the second hour Wyatt came in, accompanied by both Virgil and Morgan. He nodded to Clint and Doc, then removed the green cover from his table and began to set up for faro. That done, Morgan and Virgil left the Oriental, figuring Wyatt was safe enough there.

During the poker game Clint kept looking over at Drusilla Barnes's table, and every so often he caught her looking over at him. They'd smile at each other on those occasions and go back to their games.

The other players were all townsmen, except for one. His name was Bart Garner and he was a gambler, pure and simple. Doc had only to tell him that there was a game, and he was in it. When he arrived and discovered that he would be playing with Doc *and* Clint Adams, he was quite pleased.

The longer the game went on, the more obvious it became that the only men with a chance to be winners were Clint, Doc and Garner. The others were simply there to donate their money.

By the fourth hour, the game was indeed down to only those three. The others had either tapped out or begged off, saying they had to turn in to open their businesses early the next day.

For the next hour the three of them played just about even, so that by the end of the game they were all still ahead for the night. However, of the three men, the one who had won the most was Clint.

"I can't keep my eyes open anymore," Garner said. "Shall we continue this tomorrow night?"

"Fine with me," Clint said. "Doc?"

"Sure."

"Then goodnight, gentlemen," Bart Garner said, rising and collecting his money. "It's been a pleasure."

As Garner left Clint and Doc began to assemble their winnings.

"A beer, Doc?" Clint asked. "On me."

"Yeah, sure."

"I'll get them."

Clint stood up and walked to the bar. As he reached the bar he spotted two men, one to his left, one to his right. They were both very intent on something. Looking in the mirror behind the bar, Clint saw that what—or who—they were watching was Wyatt Earp.

"Two beers," he told Dave Brubank, who nodded.

While he waited he looked around the room, trying to see if anyone else was watching Wyatt as intently. He spotted three more men who were finding the faro table of Wyatt Earp of great interest.

Dave Brubank put the two beers on the bar just as the men to Clint's right and left began to draw their guns.

"Doc!" Clint shouted.

He threw one of the mugs of beer at the man to his left, then drew his own gun. Around the room the other three men were also drawing their weapons.

He fired, striking one of those men in the chest. He ignored the man to his right, leaving him— hopefully—for Doc Holliday.

He turned and fired at a second man, striking him high on the right side, spinning him around.

By this time Doc Holliday was up and had upended the table in front of him. He fired, killing the man to Clint's right just before the man could fire at Clint.

By now Wyatt had his gun out and fired, striking for a second time the man Clint's shot had spun around.

Clint and Doc fired at the fifth man at the same time, both shots striking him in the chest.

The shooting was over in a matter of seconds, and the silence that followed was deafening. Many of the other patrons in the saloon hadn't even had time to move or react. Now that the shooting was over they started towards the doors.

There was nothing like a good shooting to end the night's festivities.

FORTY-EIGHT

In their effort to get into the Oriental, Virgil and Morgan Earp had to fight their way through the crowd that was trying to get out. When they finally broke through they had their guns out. They saw Clint and Wyatt walking around checking bodies.

"Dead," Clint announced.

"These, too," Wyatt said.

The only others in the saloon who weren't dead were Dave Brubank and Doc Holliday. Also, standing just outside his office, was Dick Shandy.

"You Earps—," he shouted, then stopped, shook his head and abruptly went back into his office.

"Your partner doesn't look too happy," Clint said to Wyatt.

"Dave," Wyatt said, "set up some beers, would you?"

"Sure, boss."

"What happened?" Virgil asked.

"An attempted assassination," Wyatt said. "Clint and Doc broke it up."

Doc spoke up then. "It was Adams who spotted them."

"I just happened to walk to the bar when they went for their guns."

"Anybody know them?" Morgan asked.

"Not me," Wyatt said. "Doc?"

Doc hadn't seen all of them, but he shook his head anyway. Clint, newly arrived in town, had no way of knowing them, so he simply shook his head also.

"Let's take a look, Morg," Virgil said.

While Virgil and Morgan Earp were examining the dead men, the front doors opened and a man wearing a badge stepped in.

"Well, well," Wyatt said from the bar, "look who decided to put in an appearance."

"Johnny Behan," Virgil said, "as I live and breathe."

This, then, was Sheriff Johnny Behan.

"What the hell happened here?" he demanded. He was a mustached man in his late thirties, with sloping shoulders and long arms.

"What's it look like?" Wyatt asked.

"It looks like you Earps shot up another saloon," Behan said. He then added, "And your own, to boot."

"Looks like *your* friends, the Clantons, sent some incompetent help ahead of you, Behan," Virgil said. "Guess you were lookin' to come in here and find Wyatt on the floor."

"That's ridiculous," Behan objected.

"Yeah," Morgan said, "we think so, too."

Behan noticed Clint then, leaning against the bar with a beer in his hand. Doc had righted the table and was separating the money he'd picked up from the floor into two piles, his and Clint's.

"Who's that?" Behan asked. Looking directly at Clint he asked, "Who are you?"

"Somebody who happened to be in the right place at the right time," Clint answered.

The doors to the saloon opened again and two men came rushing in. From the look of them, they were Behan's deputies. They had their guns out, and Virgil and Morgan produced theirs. There was a real possibility of more gunplay, this time between the two law enforcement factions.

"Easy!" Behan shouted at his men. "Jesus, put your guns away. It's all over."

The two deputies straightened and holstered their guns.

"Now get out!" Behan snapped.

They looked at each other, then backed out through the doors.

Morgan and Virgil holstered their guns as well.

"Good move, Johnny," Morgan said.

"I don't know what happened here," Behan said, "but I don't like it."

"Neither do we," Virgil said. "Take it up with your friends, the Clantons."

"What makes you think Ike had anything to do with this?" Behan asked.

"You sure do come up with some stupid questions, Johnny," Virgil said.

"Who else would want Wyatt dead?" Morgan asked.

"Who else has been bragging they was gonna kill an Earp?" Virgil asked.

"You Earps are crazy," Behan said. "You think everybody's tryin' to kill you."

"Not everybody, Johnny," Virgil said. "Just the Clantons and the McLaurys."

"And I suppose me, too?"

"No," Virgil said, "not you, Johnny. You're friends with the Clantons, and you cover up their rustling for them, but you don't have the nerve to do any shooting yourself."

"You got no call to talk to me that way, Virgil," Behan said. "You Earps are just mad because I beat Wyatt in the election."

"It's all over here, Johnny." Wyatt spoke for the first time. "You can go, we'll clean up the mess."

"You got no authority, Wyatt," Johnny said.

"This is my place," Wyatt reminded him.

"And I *do* have authority, Johnny," Virgil said. "You best get on out, now."

John Behan stared at all of then, then pointed to Clint. "I want to see you in my office tomorrow, Mister. All strangers are required to check in with my office."

"He ain't no stranger," Morgan said.

Behan flicked a look at Morgan, then said to Clint, "Tomorrow morning." He backed out the door.

"So," Clint said, "that's the sheriff, huh?"

"You don't have to go see him, Clint," Morgan said.

"There's no harm in it, Morg," Clint said. "Besides, I don't want to give him any excuse to come down on me, or try to run me out of town."

"Let him try it and—," Morgan started, but Wyatt cut him off.

"Forget it, Morg. Clint's right. It won't do him any harm to talk to Behan."

"I'll talk to him after breakfast," Clint said. "Right now I think I've had enough excitement for one night."

"So have I," a voice said.

They all looked around and were surprised when Drusilla Barnes came out from beneath her blackjack table.

"You been under there all this time, Dru?" Wyatt asked her.

"I wasn't sure the lead had stopped flying, Boss," she said. She looked directly at Clint. "Would you mind if I left with you?"

"No," Clint said. "I'll be glad to walk you home."

"Thank you."

Clint turned to Wyatt. "You and the boys can clean this up?"

"No problem."

Clint looked across the room at Doc. "Hold my money for me, Doc, until tomorrow?" Doc waved a hand in reply.

"Miss Barnes?" Clint said. "Shall we go?"

•　•　•

Outside the saloon Clint stopped and asked, "Where do you live?"

"Down a couple of blocks," Drusilla said.

"Which way?"

She pointed. "That way."

He started to walk in the direction she had pointed. "Which way is your hotel?" she asked.

"That way," he said, pointing in the opposite direction.

"Okay," she said and started walking *that* way.

"Hey," he called.

She turned and looked at him.

"I thought you wanted me to walk you home?"

She cocked her head to one side and said to him, "I didn't say that, you did."

With that she turned back and kept walking in the direction of his hotel.

FORTY-NINE

Dressed, Drusilla Barnes looked tall and slender, cool and controlled. Naked and in bed, she was suddenly transformed into someone entirely different.

When she removed her tie and shirt, her breasts suddenly blossomed. They were large and firm, her flesh incredibly smooth and hot. When he touched her, though, she shivered and her skin became dappled with goose flesh. It was excitement and not cold that did that to her. When Clint's hands touched her body she moaned and leaned into him. She pressed her mouth to his naked shoulder and bit him. It hurt, but he didn't let her know. Instead, he lifted her into his arms and carried her to the bed.

Once in bed, she became wild and frenzied. She groped for him, tugged on him, scratched him, implored him, wrapped her legs around him and then held him tightly to her while they rocked together. He was buried deep inside her, and yet she wrapped her legs and arms around him as if she were afraid he were going to fall away from her.

He kissed her face, her mouth, her shoulders, her breasts, sucking the hard brown nipples while she held his head in her hands and groaned aloud. Waves of pleasure washed over her again and again. . . .

Later she ran her mouth over him, leaving wet trails along the way with her tongue. She kissed and bit his flesh until she worked her way down between his legs. There she cupped him in her hands, licked him, wet him thoroughly and then took him into her mouth. She was wanton and wonderful, sucking him until he thought he would explode, then releasing him and mounting him, taking him into her and sitting atop him. He grabbed her breasts while she rode him, her head thrown back to reveal the long, lovely lines of her neck. As he felt the tremors in his legs and the pressure building he squeezed her breasts harder in his hands and then she almost screamed as he exploded inside of her.

"Aren't you glad now you didn't walk me home?" she asked sometime later.

"Are you like this all the time?" Clint asked.

"Why?" she asked back. "Do you intend to be around all the time?"

"I mean—"

"I know what you mean," Dru said.

They were lying side by side on their backs. She slid one hand down over his belly and stopped at the inside of his right thigh. There she dug her nails into him. She seemed to like to use her nails and teeth, as if she were marking him as her own that way.

"I only get like that when I've been in the middle of a shooting battle," she confessed. "Jesus, I thought I was going to die right there, and I'd never feel anything like this again. It scared the hell out of me."

"So why did you pick me?"

"I didn't," she said, rubbing her palm over his thigh now.

"Oh?"

"We picked each other."

"We did?"

"Oh, yes," she said. "We would have ended up like this anyway. The fact that I thought I was going to die tonight just speeded things up a bit."

"I see," Clint said.

"Didn't you intend to take me to bed?" she asked.

"First chance I got," he admitted.

"So you see?" she said. "It would have happened sooner or later."

She slid his hand over her now, her breasts, her belly, her thighs.

"I vote for sooner," Clint said.

"The votes have already been counted," she whispered, turning towards him, her eyes shining, "and you've won."

FIFTY

The days following the assassination attempt on Wyatt Earp were anything but quiet. There was no actual violence, but there were some confrontations that could have easily erupted into violence. Actually it appeared that the Clantons were intent on avoiding that.

If, indeed, the Clantons were behind the attempt, it made sense that they would not try anything again so soon.

If, however, they were *not* involved—and it could not be definitely proven that they were—they still wouldn't want to try anything so soon after the Oriental Saloon attempt.

One thing the Oriental Saloon attempt told the town—and the Clantons—was that Clint Adams was a force to be reckoned with. It was all over town that, had it not been for Clint Adams, Wyatt Earp would be dead.

• • •

The day after the shooting Clint kept his word and went to see Sheriff John Behan.

"Didn't think you'd show," Behan said as Clint came into his office.

"I'm usually pretty law-abiding, Sheriff," Clint said, "despite what you might think."

"What I think, Adams," Behan replied, carefully placing his hands on top of his desk, "is that you'd be well advised to leave Tombstone as soon as possible."

"Are you trying to run me out of town, Sheriff?" Clint asked.

"No," Behan answered, "that's not what I'm tryin' to do, Adams. I'm tryin' to give you some advice."

"Based on what?"

"Based on your association with the Earps," Behan said. "Their luck is runnin' out, and you picked a bad time to come here and get involved with them."

"I tell you what, Sheriff," Clint told him, "if leaving town is not an order, I'd just as soon take my chances standing with the Earps . . . and Doc Holliday."

He walked to the door then and turned.

"Even if it *was* an order," he added, "I'd stay anyway. Just so you know."

Over the course of the next few days Clint and Drusilla Barnes got to know each other better and better. She came to his room each night after work, and it became known around town that they were seeing each other. Since half the men in town were in love with her, that didn't increase Clint's popularity, but he didn't care about that.

When Clint wasn't with Drusilla or in the Oriental playing poker with Doc, he was watching Wyatt's back—that is, when Doc wasn't. Morgan and Virgil kept on watching each other, while Doc and Clint took turns watching Wyatt. Wyatt watched their backs as well. The only chances anyone was taking was when Clint was with Wyatt and Doc was alone, or when Doc was with Wyatt and Clint was alone. Clint and Doc agreed, however, that the Earps were at greater risk than they were. After all, this feud was between the Clanton/McLaury faction and the Earps. Doc and Clint were simply there to back the Earps' play.

Over the course of the next few days several incidents took place.

Doc Holliday had a confrontation with Johnny Ringo in the Alhambra Saloon. The two men faced off, nearly came to blows, and then nearly drew their guns. Cooler heads, however, prevailed. Frank McLaury was with Ringo at the time, and he managed to convince Ringo to leave the saloon with him.

There was another confrontation, this time between Doc Holliday and Ike Clanton. Once again, the cooler head of the Clanton family member prevailed, as Ike backed away from Doc.

It became evident that Doc was trying to push the Clantons into something, maybe so he could kill a couple of them, thereby cutting down the odds. Each of these confrontations took place while Doc was drunk, which could also have been an explanation.

However, the Earps weren't above overreacting a bit themselves, as evidenced by an incident between them and Ike Clanton. Morgan and Virgil Earp came upon Ike Clanton quite by accident, and Ike reacted as if he thought they were going to murder him. Instead, they hit him over the head, disarmed him, dragged him to court and fined him $25.00 for carrying arms.

Only moments later Wyatt ran into Tom McLaury outside the courtroom and knocked him down with a well-timed punch. When McLaury tried to show Wyatt that he was unarmed, Wyatt pistol-whipped him and left him lying in the street.

In Clint's opinion this sort of harassment was uncalled for and only fueled the fire of the feud. The Earps, he thought, were starting to crack under the pressure and were actually starting to look like the "bad guys" to the people in town.

Even Clint himself was starting to wonder if this whole feud wasn't the Earps' own doing. Still Wyatt was his friend, and if it came to a violent confrontation, he'd have to stand with him.

And such an explosion of violence inevitably came, on October 26.

FIFTY-ONE

Clint woke with Drusilla lying on his stretched-out arm. He'd awoken that way before with other women, and his urge had always been to slide his arm from beneath their weight and then work the life back into it. This morning, though, he noticed that her weight was not unpleasant, and his arm didn't feel as if it were dead. He wondered if that meant that he was getting used to her.

That thought sobered him, brought him wide awake, and he slid his arm from beneath her head without waking her.

He walked to the window and looked down at Allen Street, which was already alive with activity. He had a strong sense of forboding that morning. It was as if he could feel the violence coming to a head, maybe even today.

He washed and dressed and left Drusilla to

sleep. They had slept together and made love together every night since the night of the Oriental Saloon shooting, but not once had they ever had breakfast together. Drusilla, working as late as she did, usually slept much later than he did, and that was fine with him. In fact, they saw each other very little during the day, spending most of their time together either in the saloon or in his room.

With the threat of violence present every moment of every day it suited him *not* to have her around. When he was trying to watch Wyatt Earp's back, he didn't need to have to watch hers as well.

He went downstairs to the hotel dining room for breakfast, knowing that very soon Wyatt and Doc would be meeting him there. In fact, once or twice Wyatt had joined him for breakfast while Doc remained outside.

Once seated in the dining room, Clint thought about Doc Holliday. He really couldn't figure the man out. He knew Doc was sick, probably dying, and that he was a singularly unpleasant man, drunk or sober. However, he could not fault the man's loyalty to Wyatt Earp—he just couldn't *understand* it. Was it merely friendship, or was there some hero worship involved? He didn't know, and he doubted that he would ever be able to figure it out.

While he was eating Wyatt appeared in the doorway and approached the table. "I've had it," Wyatt said, sitting across from his friend.

"Had what?" Clint asked.

"It!" Wyatt said. "This thing with the Clantons has got to end."

"Wyatt, we know how it's going to end, don't we?" Clint reminded him. "Do you want to push this?"

"Me?" Wyatt exploded. "Do I want to push it? Talk to the Clantons!"

"Maybe I should."

That stopped Wyatt. "Should what?"

"Talk to the Clantons," Clint answered. "Maybe I should go and talk to Ike. Try to make him see—"

"Make him see what?" asked Wyatt. "You can't talk to Ike Clanton, Clint. You can't talk to *any* of the Clantons or the McLaurys, or Johnny Ringo. You want to know what I've heard?"

"What?"

"I've heard that the Clantons have been holding Ringo back, that Ringo wants to try you. He thinks that he can take you."

"Well, maybe he can."

"I don't think so," Wyatt said. "But maybe we should start watching your back from now on, if Ringo's on the prod for you."

"I still think you and Morgan and Virgil are more at risk. I still think if I could talk to Ike—"

"Forget it, Clint," Wyatt told him. He stood up, seeming too agitated to sit any longer.

"Don't you want breakfast?" Clint asked.

"Ah," Wyatt said, "I can't eat. I'm going back outside."

"Wait for me—"

"Never mind," Wyatt said, motioning for him to remain seated. "Doc's outside. You finish your breakfast."

"Wyatt—"

"And do me a favor."

"What?"

"Stay away from the Clantons, Clint," Wyatt said. "Don't go near them alone, all right?"

"Sure, Wyatt," Clint said.

"I mean it."

"I know you do," Clint said. "I heard you, okay?"

Wyatt hesitated a moment, then said, "Okay."

He started to walk away, stopped a moment, then started again and continued until he was out the door. Clint had never seen Wyatt Earp so on edge, not even when he was a much younger man.

The sense of forboding that he had woken up with that morning was deepening.

FIFTY-TWO

Ike Clanton looked around at his brothers, the McLaury boys, Billy Claibourne and Johnny Ringo. Also, Curly Bill Brocious was with them. They were all gathered at the Clantons' shack outside of town.

"You're gonna get your chance at Clint Adams, Johnny," Ike said.

"Today?" Ringo asked anxiously.

"It's as good a day as any," Ike told him.

"Ike—," Frank McLaury began, but there was no reasoning with Ike Clanton today.

"It's too late for talk, Frank," Ike said. "The Earps have pushed this thing too far."

"But . . . they got Holliday and Adams to back their play."

"Ain't we got enough men to make up for that?" Ike asked. "Ain't we got enough guns and men who know how to use them?"

"We sure do, Ike," young Billy Clanton chimed in. "Don't worry, I'm with ya."

222

"I know you are, Billy boy," Ike said, ruffling the young man's hair. "Who else is with me?"

Frank McLaury spoke for everyone else when he said, "We're all with you, Ike. Ain't nobody here gonna back down from a fight. You know that."

"When are we gonna do it?" Johnny Ringo asked.

"Three o'clock," Ike said.

"How?" Frank asked. "Where?"

"We go into town and let the Earps know we're there, then we go over to the O.K. Corral and we wait for them there."

"What if they don't come?" Frank asked.

"They'll come."

"And what about Johnny Behan?" Tom McLaury asked. "Is he gonna be with us or with them?"

"Johnny won't be on either side," Ike said. "He's the sheriff. He won't take part in no killin'."

"Will he try to stop us?" Tom asked.

"I doubt it," Ike said. "I doubt Johnny will do anything until it's all over."

"So it's just us and them," said Billy Clanton.

"That's right, kid," Ike said. "Only it's us *or* them. After today, either we'll be gone, or the Earps will, but one way or another this thing is gonna be over."

FIFTY-THREE

After breakfast Clint went out onto the street.
It was busy, as always, but the looks on the faces
of the people he saw told him that they, too, felt
that violence was very near.

He was about to cross the street when he saw
Sheriff Behan approaching. He waited there for
the man to catch up to him.

"Adams," Behan called, as if Clint hadn't seen
him.

"What can I do for you today, Sheriff?"

Behan joined him on the boardwalk in front of
the hotel. "I don't like the way it feels today,"
Behan said. "Do you feel it?"

Clint hunched his shoulders, hating to agree
with the man. "Yes," he said finally. "I feel it,
Sheriff. There's something bad in the air."

"It's gonna happen today," Behan said. "I can
feel it in my bones."

"Maybe we can stop it," Clint suggested.

"How?"

"By talking to the Clantons."

"Me?"

"No," Clint said. "I was thinking of me."

"How could you get near enough to them to talk?" he asked. "If you go out to their place they'll probably shoot you on sight."

Clint looked at Behan. "Not if you go with me."

"Me?" Behan said. "What makes you think they won't shoot me, too?"

"Come on, Behan," Clint said. "You and the Clantons are friends, aren't you?"

"Well," Behan said, "we're *friendly*—"

"You can get me close enough to talk to Ike," Clint said. "Maybe I can convince him that there's another way out of this."

"Can't you convince Earp?" Behan asked.

"No," Clint said, "I can't."

"So what makes you think Ike will listen to you when your own friend won't?"

"I don't know, Sheriff," Clint replied. "I only know that if I don't try and blood is shed I won't feel that I did everything I could to stop it."

Behan thought it over.

"Come on, Sheriff," Clint said, "do you really want them to turn Tombstone into a blood bath? Do you want them to put Tombstone in the history books for all the wrong reasons? After all, it's your town, isn't it? You're the sheriff."

Behan ran his hand over his face. "All right," he said, "all right. I'll take you out there, and I'll try to keep you alive, but I can't guarantee that Ike will listen to you."

"Good enough," Clint said. "Let's get going."

"Now?" Behan asked.

"Now's as good a time as ever, Sheriff," Clint answered. "Isn't it?"

Behan made a face. "I suppose so," he said.

When Ike Clanton saw the two riders approaching he couldn't believe his eyes. What the hell was Johnny Behan doing with Clint Adams? Ike ducked inside his shack to get his rifle and then came back out. He was alone. His brothers and the McLaurys had left, as had Ringo, Claibourne and Brocious. They were going to meet up later in town, but for now Ike Clanton was all alone.

He stood his ground on his porch, his rifle held in both hands, pointing at Behan and Clint Adams as they reined their horses in.

"What the hell is this, Sheriff?" Ike asked.

"Ike, settle down," Behan said. "Put that rifle up."

"Not until you tell me why you brought him out here," Ike said, using the rifle to point to Clint.

"He just wants to talk, Ike," Behan said. "That's all, just some talk."

"Okay," Ike said, "if he wants to talk have him hand you his gun, and then I'll talk."

"I hand him my gun," Clint said, "what's my guarantee you won't blow me out of my saddle?"

Before Ike could answer Behan said, "He'll put up his rifle, won't you, Ike?"

Ike gave Behan a hard stare.

"I won't have you shootin' an unarmed man in front of me, Ike," Behan said. "I won't have that."

Ike thought it over and then lowered the rifle. Clint removed his gun from his holster—against his better judgment—and handed it to Behan.

"Ike," Behan said.

Ike hesitated, then put the rifle down on the porch.

"Okay," he said, folding his arms. "Talk, Adams."

"Ike," Clint said, "this thing between you and Wyatt—between your family and the Earps—can only end in bloodshed."

"I know that," Ike said, "and so do the Earps. We all know that, Adams. What's your point?"

"The point, Ike," Clint replied, "is to avoid it."

"Why?"

Clint stared at the man for a moment, not sure he'd heard him right. "To keep anyone from getting killed," he finally said. Surely anyone could appreciate that, right?

"It's too late for that," Ike said. "Did Wyatt Earp send you out here to plead for him?"

"You know better than that, Ike. Wyatt would never plead. I'm here on my own, to try and keep you from killing each other."

"Well," Ike said, "like I told you, it's too late for that. It's too late for talk."

"Ike—"

"That's all," Ike said. "I'm through listening."

Ike picked up his rifle and went into the shack.

Looking at Ike Clanton's face just then had given Clint a chill. The look on the man's face was the same look he had seen on Wyatt's face that morning in the dining room.

These men were intent on killing each other, and no amount of talking was going to change that.

Clint and Sheriff Behan rode back to town in silence, not speaking until they had put their horses up at the O.K. Corral livery.

"Thanks for taking me out there, Behan," Clint said. "I had to try."

Behan shook his head. "I never thought it would go this far, Adams," he said. "Believe me."

"And if it goes further?"

"Whataya mean?" Behan asked.

"If they come to town intent on killing each other, are you going to try and stop them?"

"I got two deputies, Adams," Behan said. "You think they're gonna be willing to get between the Earps and the Clantons for what this town pays them?"

"I'm not asking you about your deputies," Clint said. "I'm asking about you, Sheriff."

Behan hesitated a moment and then said, "I'll do what I can, Adams. I ain't a coward, but I'm not about to get killed, either. Does that answer your question?"

"It's good enough, I guess," Clint said. "I guess all we can do now is wait and see what happens."

FIFTY-FOUR

1:00 P.M.

Clint Adams was with the Earps and Doc
Holliday at Campbell and Hatch's Billiard Parlor. Morgan and Virgil were playing, while Wyatt
and Clint watched. Doc was sitting by the window,
looking outside.

The general opinion was that something was
definitely going to happen today, so they had
decided to all stay together during the afternoon.

Clint noticed at one point that Wyatt was staring at him.

"You did it, didn't you?" Wyatt finally asked.

"Did what?"

"You know what," Wyatt said. "You went out
and talked to Ike Clanton, didn't you?"

It occurred to him to lie, but he decided against
it.

"Yes, Wyatt, I did."

"And what happened?"

"Nothing," Clint said. "He's as intent on killing you as you are on killing him."

"I told you," Wyatt said, "the time for talk is past."

"That's what he said."

"Well, for once me and Ike Clanton agree on something," said Wyatt.

Clint just shook his head.

"Look, Clint," Wyatt began. "I'll tell you the same thing I told Doc. You can pull out anytime with no hard feelings. I know that this is crazy, and stupid, and shouldn't happen, but it's beyond stopping. Virgil, Morg and me, we're trapped, but you and Doc ain't."

"What did Doc say?"

"Doc's staying."

"I'm staying too, Wyatt," Clint told him.

"Clint," Wyatt said, "it's different with Doc, but you—"

"I know about Doc, Wyatt. But I'm not about to ride out, especially not today."

"What is it about today?" Wyatt asked. "Everybody feels it. You, me, Doc, Morg and Virg, even the people on the streets."

"There's death in the air," Clint replied. "You can usually smell that."

"I guess," Wyatt said. He looked over at Doc. "What's the street look like, Doc?"

"Quiet," Doc said.

"Any sign of the Clantons?"

"No," Doc said, then added, "there's *nobody* on the street."

"Everybody expectin' trouble," Morg said, looking up from the table.

"I heard Ike got himself some more help." Virgil straightened up without making the shot he was lining up.

"Who?" Wyatt asked.

"Billy Claibourne," Virgil said, "also Curly Bill Brocious."

"I seen Brocious around with Ringo," Morgan told them, "but I didn't think nothin' of it."

"Today?" Virgil asked.

"Yeah."

"I didn't see them."

"Well, I did."

"Why didn't you tell me—?"

"Ringo's mine," Doc said, interrupting them.

Somehow word had gotten around that Ringo had been seeing Kate Elder. Suddenly Doc considered Kate his and was intent on killing Ringo.

"When the time comes," Wyatt said, "I don't think we're going to be able to pick and choose who we want to shoot, Doc."

"Maybe not," Doc said, "maybe not. . . ." But he didn't sound convinced.

"Wyatt," Clint suggested, "let's go for a little walk."

"Where?"

"Just outside."

Wyatt shrugged and followed Clint outside. Out in front of the pool hall Clint stopped and faced Wyatt.

"Doc's too intent on Ringo, Wyatt," Clint said.

"That can get him killed, and you killed, in a shootout."

"I know it," Wyatt said, "but what can I do?"

"Morgan said he saw Brocious and Ringo around together," Clint said. "Maybe I can keep them out of the play."

"Clint," Wyatt replied, "we don't even know if there *is* going to be a play today."

"Oh, I think we do."

Wyatt thought a moment. "To do that," he said, "you'll have to get the drop on them—and if you're going to keep them out of the play, that keeps you out of it, too."

"I know," Clint said, "but it would cut down on the odds, and Doc wouldn't have Ringo to fix on."

Wyatt thought some more. Then he nodded and said, "All right, it makes sense. Go ahead and do it. I'll go back upstairs and wait with the boys."

Clint looked out at the street. For the time of the day it was deserted.

"Be careful, Wyatt," he said.

"You, too," Wyatt replied. "See you later."

Wyatt went back upstairs, and Clint went looking for Johnny Ringo, whom he knew on sight, and Curly Bill Brocious, whom he did not.

FIFTY-FIVE

1:30 P.M.

"Wyatt," Doc said from the window.

"What is it, Doc?"

"The McLaurys just rode down the street with Billy Claibourne."

Wyatt moved to the window, but they were gone from view already.

"Where'd they go?" he asked.

"Towards the O.K. Corral."

"Any sign of the Clantons?" Wyatt asked. "Ike?"

"No," Doc said, "not yet."

Wyatt put his hand on his friend's shoulder. "Nothing's going to happen until the Clantons get here," Wyatt told him. "Not until Ike is here."

"Well, at least we know something is gonna happen," Doc said. "With Brocious and Ringo in town, and now the McLaurys and Billy Claibourne."

"I wish it would happen soon," Virgil said from the pool table.

Although he and Morgan had been playing pool

233

the whole time, neither of them was paying much attention to the game. Hell, they weren't even playing for money.

"Where's Clint?" Morgan asked, as if he'd just noticed that he was gone.

"He had something to do."

Doc looked a question at Wyatt, who simply shook his head. He didn't want to tell Doc what Clint was doing. Doc was so intent on killing Ringo, there was no predicting what he'd do.

"Let me know when you see Ike," Wyatt said. "That's when it will be time to go."

Clint had wandered around town for half an hour, poking his head into the Alhambra, the Oriental and some of the other saloons and hotels, looking for Johnny Ringo and Curly Brocious. At one point he saw the three riders who had come to town. The only one he recognized was Frank McLaury, whom he had seen once or twice. He watched as they rode down Allen Street, past the pool hall, and continued on towards the O.K. Corral. He knew that Doc Holliday must have seen them, so he and the Earps knew that things were starting to happen.

He renewed his search for Ringo and the other man. He had to find them before the Clantons arrived. When Ike and his brothers got there, that would signal the beginning—the beginning of who knew how much bloodshed and death.

At five minutes to two Sheriff Johnny Behan appeared on the street in front of the pool hall.

"Sheriff's on the way," Doc said.

"He's too late," Wyatt said.

Morgan and Virgil had abandoned any pretense of playing pool and were just sitting around, holding their pool sticks. Now they stood up and set the sticks aside. Wyatt, too, was standing when Behan walked in.

"Wyatt," he said.

"Johnny."

"Ike and the boys are at the O.K. Corral," Behan said.

Wyatt looked at Doc. "They didn't pass this way," Doc said.

"No," Behan said. "They came into town by another route."

"Is Ringo with them?" Doc asked.

"Not yet," Behan said, "but he will be—him and Brocious." Behan looked around curiously. "Where's Adams?"

"He'll be around."

"Even with him you're outnumbered, Wyatt," Behan warned.

"It's not how many guns you have, Sheriff," Wyatt said, "it's what you do with them."

Doc stood up and picked up the shotgun he'd had on the floor next to him. "Wyatt," he said.

"I know," Wyatt Earp said. "It's time."

"Can I stop you, Wyatt?" Behan asked.

"No, Johnny," Wyatt said, "and if I were you I wouldn't try."

"I'll walk over with you, then," Behan said.

"You takin' sides, Sheriff?" Virgil asked.

"No sides," Behan said. "I'll have to be on hand to arrest the survivors—that is, unless you're goin' over there to arrest the Clantons and the others, Virgil."

"Those men have made their threats," Virgil said. "I am not going to arrest them, I am going to shoot them on sight."

Johnny Behan shook his head but said nothing.

"Ready boys?" Wyatt asked his brothers.

"We're ready," Virgil said.

"Doc?"

"Let's get to it," Doc said. "There's killin' to be done."

FIFTY-SIX

It was a little after two o'clock when Wyatt, Morgan and Virgil Earp starting walking towards the O.K. Corral with Doc Holliday and John Behan. The walked down Freemont, which was not only one of the widest streets in town, but the dustiest as well. The corral extended from Allen Street to Fremont Street, so that it could be reached from either side. As the Earps reached the corral they realized that the Clantons and their gang were on the Allen Street side.

"I see Billy Claibourne with them," Doc Holliday said. "I don't see Ringo."

"No," Wyatt said. "Neither do I."

"Johnny," Virgil said to Behan, "this might be a good time for you to find someplace else to be."

"Yeah," Behan said, "I think you're right."

"Sure," Morgan said with a sneer. "Come on back when it's time to pick up the pieces."

Behan pointed a finger at Morgan. "You don't know what you're talkin' about, boy. It don't take courage to fight, it takes courage *not* to fight."

"Yeah," Morgan said to Behan's retreating back, "you keep believing that."

Clint heard the talk on the street that the Clantons were already at the O.K Corral, and the Earps were on their way. It suddenly occurred to him that maybe the Clantons were setting a trap. Since they had gotten to the corral first, they could have set up anything.

Clint started down Allen Street on the run. When he came into view of the corral he saw the Clantons and the McLaurys standing together. He also saw something at the door to C. S. Fly's Photograph Gallery: the door was ajar. Of course, it was possible that the proprietor had fled in haste and left it open, but Clint decided to take a look.

He moved up to the door of the gallery and stepped inside very quietly. Standing at a window from which he could see the entire corral was Johnny Ringo. Next to him another man stood, and Clint assumed that this was Curly Bill Brocious.

"So this is it, eh?" Clint asked aloud. "An ambush."

Ringo and Brocious froze, and Ringo lifted his shoulders up high, as if something cold were wending its way down his back.

"I'd heard a lot about you, Ringo," Clint said, "but never that you were a bushwhacker."

"Adams?" Ringo asked.

"That's right."

Ever so slowly Curly Brocious was moving his hand towards his holstered gun.

"Keep going, Curly," Clint said. "It'll be the last thing you ever do."

"Take it easy," Ringo said to Brocious. "He'll kill you, and me, too."

"But, the fight—"

"We're all going to watch the fight," Clint told them, "from right here. Boys, take out your guns, tips of the fingers of the left hand, please."

Ringo and Brocious—both right-handed—obeyed.

"On the floor."

They dropped their guns to the floor.

"All right," Clint said. "Now let's watch what happens, shall we? Now that the odds have evened out a little."

Helplessly Ringo and Brocious looked out at the O.K. Corral. There was nothing they could do. They could only hope that their friends would be the survivors.

FIFTY-SEVEN

On their side of the corral the Earps spread out, and on the other side of the Clanton gang did the same.

Since Virgil was the marshal, he was the one who spoke first. "Throw up your hands!"

And the shooting started.

Doc leveled his shotgun and let go with both barrels. He did not stop to see what effect his shots had. He discarded the shotgun, produced his six-gun and began to fire.

Finn Clanton was the first to fall, as Doc's double-barrel blast caught him full in the midsection, almost cutting him in half.

The next to die was Tom McLaury, and it was difficult for bystanders—for there were a few, Clint Adams among them—to say who had shot him. Lead was flying all over by now, with everyone shooting.

Of all the men in the corral Ike Clanton would have been the one least expected to bolt. Ike was the one who had seemed most in favor of the feud ending this way. But now that the shooting had started Ike bolted and ran for the photograph gallery.

As the man entered Clint turned and pointed his gun at him.

"Ringo!" Ike called, then stopped when he saw Clint Adams.

"No help for you in here, Clanton," Clint said. He felt no compassion for the man, as he had obviously set a trap for the Earps that had fallen through.

"Adams," Ike said, "listen—"

"Outside, Ike," Clint said, "or I'll shoot you right here."

"Damn you!" Ike Clanton shouted, running back outside.

During this time Frank McLaury had been killed and Billy Claibourne had cut and run. Morgan Earp was down with a bullet in his shoulder, and Clint could see from the window that Wyatt was crouched over him, shielding him.

Ike Clanton ran directly for Wyatt Earp and grabbed his arm. "Don't kill me," Ike shouted. "I ain't doin' no shootin'."

Angrily Wyatt shook the man off, knocking him to the ground. "Goddamn you, this fight's begun," Wyatt shouted. "Get to fighting, or get out."

Wyatt wanted Ike to go for his gun. Even in the heat of battle he could not shoot a man who would not defend himself. This time, however, he should have made an exception.

"Wyatt, look out!"

Wyatt heard Morgan's warning and turned in time to see a wounded Billy Clanton bearing down on him. Morgan pushed himself up to a seated position and fired, striking the already wounded man in the stomach. Billy Clanton screamed and fell back.

Wyatt looked around for Ike Clanton, but the older Clanton brother was long gone. He suddenly realized that the shooting had stopped. Frank and Tom McLaury were dead, as was Finn Clanton. Morgan was down with a bullet in his shoulder, and Virgil with a wound to his leg. Billy Clanton, shot twice—once in the gut—was still alive, but the youngster would not last much longer.

Doc Holliday was standing, ejecting shells from his handgun and reloading it.

"It's over, Doc!" Wyatt called.

Doc nodded but did not put up his gun. Instead, he began to inspect the bodies one by one.

Wyatt knew he was looking for Ringo.

Inside Fly's Photograph Gallery Ringo said, "It's over, Adams."

"Your side lost, Ringo."

"Let me have my gun," Ringo said. "Come on, Adams, you and me."

"I don't think so, Ringo," Clint replied. "I think you and Curly should be on your way."

"You ain't gonna kill us?" Brocious asked in disbelief.

"No."

"You're lettin' us go?" said Ringo.

"As long as you promise to leave town," Clint said. "If I see you back here again—"

"You'll see me again, Adams," Ringo promised, "not back here, but you'll see me."

"Be on your way, boys," Clint said, "and don't think about coming back."

Brocious went out the door first, and Ringo followed, throwing one last murderous glance back at Clint.

"Another place, Adams," Ringo said. "Another time and place." He turned and followed Brocious away from the O.K. Corral.

Clint stepped out of the gallery behind them, then turned and walked into the corral.

FIFTY-EIGHT

After it was all over there were people running every which way, coming to see what the commotion had wrought.

Clint entered the corral and walked up to Wyatt. "You all right?" he asked.

"Yes," Wyatt said. "Morg and Virg been hit, though. Doc's fine. He's looking for Ringo."

Clint turned and saw Doc leaning over a body.

"Ringo's gone, Wyatt," Clint said. He explained that he had thrown down on Ringo and Brocious in the photographic gallery and held them there until the fighting was over, then let them go.

"Just as well," Wyatt said. He looked down at Morgan. "How you doin', Morg?"

"I'll live," Morgan said. "How's Virgil?"

"I'll find out," Clint told him.

"Thanks," Wyatt said, and leaned over Morgan.

Clint walked over to where Virgil was sitting on the ground. There were a few men gathered around him, and one was probing a wound in his leg.

"You a doctor?" Clint asked.

"That's right."

A woman appeared then. It was Allie, Virgil's wife. The crowd wanted to hold her back, but she would have none of it. She eventually broke through and rushed to her husband's side.

"Virg!"

"I'm fine," Virgil told her, "or I would be if this damn fool doctor would stop poking me."

"I can't find the bullet," the doctor complained.

Clint leaned over to take a look. He abruptly grabbed the doctor's probing hand and pulled it away. "That's because the bullet went clean through the calf."

The doctor bent lower to take a look, then straightened up. "Oh," he said.

"Move out of the way," Clint said, annoyed. The man was obviously incompetent.

"Can we take him home?" Allie Earp asked.

"Sure," Clint said. "Come on, some of you lift him up and carry him to his house."

"How's Morgan?" Virgil asked.

"He's got a shoulder wound."

"Bring him to the house, too," Allie directed.

"I'll arrange it," Clint said.

She put her hand on his arm and said, "Thank you."

So they carried Virgil and Morgan Earp to Virgil's house, where they were deposited side-by-side on the same bed.

"What's going to happen now?" Allie asked her husband.

"I don't know," Virgil said. He was annoyed with himself for having gotten shot.

Presently both Wyatt and Clint came to the Earp house to see how Virgil and Morgan were. Doc Holliday had gone off somewhere. They had both lost track of him.

"What's it like out there, Wyatt?" Morgan asked.

"It's crazy," Wyatt said. "Johnny Behan says he's gonna arrest us for murder."

"What did you tell him?" Virgil asked.

"I told him we would not be arrested!"

"Good!" Morgan said.

"Clint and I will try to see to it that nobody bothers you boys while you recuperate."

"What happened to Doc?" Virgil asked.

"I don't know," Wyatt replied. He hoped that Doc was not still looking for Johnny Ringo.

"Is there another doctor in town?" Clint asked. "Besides that idiot who was poking Virgil's leg?"

"Doc Potter," Wyatt answered. "He's old, but he's good."

"We'd better fetch him, then," Clint said. "These boys need looking after."

"We'll get the doctor," Wyatt told his brothers, "and then we'll talk to Johnny Behan."

"Give 'im hell, Wyatt," Morgan Earp said through teeth clenched in pain.

After finding the doctor and sending him off to the Earp house, they went to the sheriff's office to talk to Johnny Behan. On the way they passed the hardware store. Already the bodies of the dead men had been dressed in all kinds of finery and propped up in the window. A sign above the bodies said, THESE MEN WERE MURDERED IN COLD BLOOD.

"Think they're tryin' to tell us something?" Wyatt asked.

"Forget it, Wyatt," Clint said. "Everybody has friends."

"Even scum like that," Wyatt added.

They reached Behan's office and entered without knocking. Behan, who was standing by his desk when they entered, whirled and glared at them. Clint had a feeling that the man wanted to go for his gun but dared not.

It was a good choice.

FIFTY-NINE

"We're not here for any trouble, Sheriff," Clint said. "We just want to straighten this whole thing out."

Behan didn't look at Clint, he looked at Wyatt. "Wyatt, I gotta arrest you and your brothers. It's my job."

"And if Ike and his boys were still standing?" Wyatt asked. "Would you arrest them?"

"Well . . . sure."

"Well, they ain't all dead, you know," Wyatt said. "Why don't you go out and look for them? For Ike and Ringo and the others?"

Behan hesitated a moment. "My deputies are out now, lookin', but I got you and your brothers right here, Wyatt."

"We won't be arrested, Johnny," Wyatt informed him.

Behan compressed his lips for a moment, then decided to try another tack. "How are Morgan and Virgil?"

"Bad," Wyatt said. "I won't let you put them in a cell."

"Well," Behan said thoughtfully, "if they're hurt they surely ain't goin' nowhere. There'll have to be a trial, Wyatt. After all, Virgil is a marshal."

Clint kept his eye on Wyatt. With Virgil sworn to uphold the law, the Earps would have to abide by it. Behan was right. There would have to be a trial.

"I've got an idea," Clint said.

Both men looked at him. Wyatt asked, "What?"

"What if the sheriff arrested you and the boys," he said, "but he didn't put you in a cell."

"What are you talkin' about?" Behan asked.

"Morgan and Virgil aren't going anywhere, Sheriff," Clint said. "You just said so yourself. What if Wyatt agrees not to leave town. They'll all three be here when the judge arrives."

Behan looked at Wyatt. "What do you say, Wyatt?"

"I don't want Doc Holliday arrested," Wyatt said, "or Clint, here. Just me and my brothers. It was our fight."

"I don't know if I can let Doc off—"

"You want to try to take Doc in, Johnny?" Wyatt asked. "He won't come as easy as me, you know that."

Behan thought a moment, then nodded. "Okay. I won't arrest Doc or Adams. You and your brothers will stand trial willingly?"

"Right," Wyatt agreed.

"All right, then," Behan said. "It's done."

"Done," Wyatt said, and he and Clint left the office.

Outside Wyatt said, "We should just ride out of town tonight."

"You can't do that Wyatt, and you know it," Clint said. "Morgan and Virgil can't ride."

"I could put them in a buckboard."

"It would still be too much for them," Clint said. "Besides, you know you can't leave. You and the boys would be on the run."

"I know." Wyatt looked across the street at the window of the hardware store, where the dead bodies had been propped. "Do you think we'll get a fair trial in Tombstone? A lot of people have it in for us, you know."

"That doesn't matter," Clint said. "It'll be up to a judge, not up to the people."

"Well," Wyatt said, "after we're found innocent, I'm getting out of this town. I'm sure Morgan and Virgil will feel the same way."

"I can't say that I blame you," Clint told his friend. "I'd leave, too."

Wyatt looked at Clint. "You can leave now, you know," he said. "There's no reason for you to stay around."

"Wyatt—"

"No, I mean it," Wyatt said. "Besides, Behan might change his mind about arresting you. If you're gone, he'll forget about you."

"What about you and the boys?"

"What good can you do us here, Clint?" Wyatt

asked. "Besides, I really don't want you to see me standing trial."

Clint eyed his friend. "If you put it that way—"

"I do," Wyatt said. He put his hand on Clint's shoulder. "I appreciate your help. If you hadn't taken Ringo out of the fight things might have gone differently. Thank you."

"No reason to thank me," Clint said. "I did what any friend would have done."

"I don't think it's that simple," Wyatt said. "Now do yourself a favor."

"What?"

"Get out of this town tomorrow," Wyatt replied. "Put Tombstone as far behind you as you can. We'll meet up again somewhere after this is all over."

"Somewhere quiet," Clint said.

"Right," Wyatt said. "Maybe Canada."

"Canada's nice."

"Or Alaska."

"I've been to both places," Clint said. "They're—nice."

"Okay, then," said Wyatt. "Let's go and tell the boys they're under arrest."

SIXTY

Clint was in no hurry to get back to Labyrinth, Texas. Along the way he followed the progress of the hearing through the newspapers. The hearing would decide whether or not there was to be a trial.

The "Gunfight at the O.K. Corral," as the papers were calling it, had commanded a lot of attention, and so too had the aftermath.

Through the various newspaper accounts Clint learned that Virgil had been fired as marshal by the city fathers. He and Morgan remained in Virgil's house during the trial, while Wyatt Earp and Doc Holliday went to the courtroom every day. It was not clear to Clint whether or not Doc had been arrested. If he had, it would mean that Johnny Behan had lied. Wyatt had been right to tell Clint to leave. He might be on trial right along with them if he hadn't.

Of course, Doc being such a good friend to Wyatt, and loyal, there was always the chance

252

that he had given himself up and simply agreed to stand trial along with his friend.

The trial took up the whole month of November.

What Clint did not know was the fear that existed in the Earp household during that month. Threats were made against the Earps' lives, and both Morgan and Virgil kept their guns handy while laid up in bed. The Earp wives—Lou and Allie, respectively—hardly ever left the house, and they all simply waited at the house for word from Wyatt and Doc as to how they were doing at the hearing.

There were many witnesses during the hearing, so many that Wyatt and Doc wondered where all these people had been during the actual shooting.

For the most part townspeople testified that the Clantons and McLaurys were unarmed. One witness swore that Frank McLaury was unarmed when he was in his store, just before the fight; another claimed that Tom McLaury had left his gun with him, and that he still had it; and yet another claimed to have heard Virgil's statement about killing the Clantons on sight. More than one person testified that the first two shots were fired by Morgan Earp and Doc Holliday, almost simultaneously; and Sheriff Johnny Behan testified that Ike Clanton had thrown up his arms just before the fight commenced, and also later asked Wyatt not to kill him, because he wasn't shooting.

There were, of course, witnesses for the Earps. One was a judge who had watched the fight from the courthouse, and another a woman who ran a hat shop. Both claimed to have seen all the parties involved firing weapons, including the Clantons.

Ike Clanton also testified, saying that his brothers' and Frank McLaury's hands were up and that Tom McLaury was throwing open his coat to show that he was unarmed when the shooting started.

Finally Wyatt Earp himself testified, reading from a long, prepared statement. He recounted the history between the Earps and the Clantons, tracing the entire matter back to the theft of six government mules from Camp Rucker. He testified that he, Morgan and Doc Holliday had been sworn in as U.S. deputy marshals by Marshal Virgil Earp, and were therefore doing their jobs when the fight at the O.K. Corral took place.

Clint was able to follow most of this through the newspapers he read along the way and through the accounts he read upon arriving back in Labyrinth, Texas.

On December 1 the judge presiding over the hearing—Judge Spicer—rendered his decision.

His statement was long and involved, and maintained that there was enough testimony to indicate that the Clantons and McLaurys reacted to demands of surrender by producing their weapons, and that shots were fired from both sides almost instantaneously. He also stated that he could not resist the conviction that if indeed the Earps had fired first, just a second or seconds before the Clantons, they had acted wisely in their decision to do so, in that firing the first shots was necessary to save their own lives.

There being no sufficient evidence to bind them over for trial, the judge declared the defendants—Wyatt, Morgan and Virgil Earp, and Doc Holliday—to be released.

The Earps, however, did not leave Tombstone immediately. They could not. The convalescence of Morgan and Virgil was lengthy, although Morgan was up and around before Virgil was.

In March Morgan was out and around when Virgil and Allie Earp heard shots. "Run, Allie," Virgil shouted. "Go and see who it is now."

Allie ran and saw that a big crowd had jammed into Campbell and Hatch's billiard place. She pushed her way into the place and had to climb up into a pool table to see what was happening. That was when she saw Wyatt Earp and his brother Warren—who had not been involved in the O.K. Corral shooting—bending over a fallen Morgan.

Warren saw Allie and shouted, "For God's sake, Al, go home!"

She ran back to get Virgil, who was being helped to dress by the doctor. It was the first time he had been up in three months. By the time she and Virgil returned to Hatch's, Morgan had been lifted onto a couch. A bullet had entered his spine, and he did not have long to live.

He opened his eyes at one point and asked, "Are my legs stretched out and my boots on?"

Everyone nodded . . . and Morgan Earp died.

According to Bob Hatch himself, Morgan had stopped to have a game of billiards with him. Wyatt Earp and some others were watching. Morgan's back was to the back door, and while Hatch was bent over to make a shot, the back door crashed open and a shot sounded. Morgan spun around, but then fell to the ground. A second shot missed him, but the first had done its job.

It was assumed that Morgan Earp was gunned down in retaliation for the O.K. Corral incident.

The Earps left Tombstone shortly after Morgan's death.

EPILOGUE

EL PASO, TEXAS
THE FOLLOWING YEAR
SEPTEMBER 19, 1882

Clint had read about the acquittal of the Earps.
In March of the following year he had read about
the assassination of Morgan Earp. After that, he
lost track of the Earps and Doc Holliday, but
he knew that he and Wyatt would cross paths
again, soon, and he would hear the rest of the
story then.

Meanwhile, he had lost track of Dallas Stoudenmire and the goings-on in El Paso. During
the hearing about the O.K. Corral and the entire
aftermath of that incident, there was little room
in some of the smaller western newspapers for
anything else. Since El Paso had continued to
exist quietly for a while, it eventually fell from
the pages of the newspapers—and from the mind
of Clint Adams.

• • •

In September of the year following the O.K. Corral, Clint found himself a day or two's ride from El Paso, and he decided to ride over and visit with Dallas Stoudenmire. He hoped that things had remained sufficiently calm in El Paso since his last visit, that maybe the feud with the Mannings had blown over.

He had seen firsthand the tragedy that could occur because of a feud, and he hoped that Dallas Stoudenmire would be able to avoid that.

On September 19, Clint rode into El Paso and found the town to be unchanged, at least to the naked eye. It had not progressed or regressed in any obvious way.

He rode to the marshal's office, but the door was locked and no one answered his knock.

He then rode to the Top Dollar Saloon, left Duke outside and went in. The same bartender he had met last year was there behind the bar, elbows resting on it. There was but one man in the place, and Clint swore it was the same man seated at the same table as last year. He wondered if he was working on the same drink.

"Beer," Clint said to the bartender.

The man jerked up off the bar, startled, and then looked closely at Clint. "I know you," he said.

"Beer," Clint said.

The man drew the beer and set it in front of Clint. "You were here last year."

"That's right."

"You helped the marshal stand against—"

"That's right, I did," Clint said. "I just rode in to see Marshal Stoudenmire. He's not at his office. Do you know where he is?"

"Sure do."

"Where?"

"He's at the undertaker's."

Clint closed his eyes. "Was there trouble?" he asked. "Did he have to kill somebody?"

The man frowned. "Are you a friend of his?" he asked.

"I consider myself to be, yes," Clint replied.

"Then I am sorry to tell you," the bartender said, "that your friend was shot and killed yesterday."

At 5:30 p.m., September 18, Dallas Stoudenmire met with Doc Manning in Frank Manning's saloon to meet and discuss the feud, which was still going on.

Witnesses stated that the two men argued and then stood up. Another man stepped between them and Doc Manning took this opportunity to pull his gun and fire. The bullet ripped through Dallas Stoudenmire's arm and chest as the marshal drew his own gun.

Doc Manning charged Stoudenmire and fired again at his chest, but they said that some papers and a photograph in his pocket kept the bullet from penetrating his body.

From there the two men staggered outside and

began to grapple. Stoudenmire produced a small belly gun and shot Doc Manning in the arm, causing Manning to drop his gun, and the men continued to wrestle.

At this point Jim Manning came running up with his .45 drawn. He fired at Stoudenmire but missed. He stepped closer then, virtually putting the gun behind Stoudenmire's left ear, and fired, killing him.

"After that," the bartender said, "Doc Manning picked up the marshal's gun and started pistol-whipping his body. It was an ugly sight."

Clint listened to the entire story, his body growing colder and colder. First Morgan Earp was killed as a by-product of the Earp-Clanton feud, and now Dallas Stoudenmire was dead—the very day before Clint arrived.

It was tempting to think that if he had been there he could have saved Stoudenmire, but then what would have happened the next time? That kind of thinking was just futile, Clint knew.

"Where are the Mannings now?" he asked.

"They're under arrest," the bartender said. A marshal named Gillette showed up this mornin'. He took them into custody."

Clint nodded. As cold and sad as he felt, oddly enough he felt no desire for revenge. "Thanks for the beer," he said.

"Sure thing," the bartender said, and Clint left the Top Dollar.

• • •

Clint rode down to the undertaker's, but outside he did not dismount. He debated as to whether or not he really wanted to see Stoudenmire's body, then decided that it would change nothing either way.

As for the Mannings, they were in custody and it would be a matter of time before they paid for their crime—if, indeed, they did. That was just something else he was going to have to follow through the newspapers.

He turned Duke north, rode out of El Paso, and never went back.

AUTHOR'S NOTE

Certain liberties have been taken with the historical characters and incidents depicted in this book. This is not meant to be a true and accurate account of the O.K. Corral incident, or the Dallas Stoudenmire/El Paso incident, but rather fictionalized versions in which Clint Adams, the Gunsmith, could easily have taken part.

Watch for

GILA RIVER CROSSING

143rd novel in the exciting GUNSMITH series
from Jove

Coming in November!

If you enjoyed this book, subscribe now and get...

TWO FREE

A $7.00 VALUE—

A special offer for people who enjoy reading the best Westerns published today.

WESTERNS!

NO OBLIGATION

Mail the coupon below

To start your subscription and receive 2 FREE WESTERNS, fill out the coupon below and mail it today. We'll send your first shipment which includes 2 FREE BOOKS as soon as we receive it.

Mail To: **True Value Home Subscription Services, Inc. P.O. Box 5235
120 Brighton Road, Clifton, New Jersey 07015-5235**

YES! I want to start reviewing the very best Westerns being published today. Send me my first shipment of 6 Westerns for me to preview FREE for 10 days. If I decide to keep them, I'll pay for just 4 of the books at the low subscriber price of $2.75 each; a total $11.00 (a $21.00 value). Then each month I'll receive the 6 newest and best Westerns to preview Free for 10 days. If I'm not satisfied I may return them within 10 days and owe nothing. Otherwise I'll be billed at the special low subscriber rate of $2.75 each; a total of $16.50 (at least a $21.00 value) and save $4.50 off the publishers price. There are never any shipping, handling or other hidden charges. I understand I am under no obligation to purchase any number of books and I can cancel my subscription at any time, no questions asked. In any case the 2 FREE books are mine to keep.

Name _____

Street Address _____ Apt. No. _____

City _____ State _____ Zip Code _____

Telephone _____

Signature _____

(if under 18 parent or guardian must sign)

Terms and prices subject to change. Orders subject
to acceptance by True Value Home Subscription
Services, Inc.   11212-7